THE SHOP OF THE LIN FAMILY
&
SPRING SILKWORMS

中國現代文學中英對照系列
Bilingual Series on Modern Chinese Literature

本系列已出版書籍 Published Titles in the Series

《寒夜》 *Cold Nights* (2002)
巴金著　茅國權、柳存仁英譯
By Ba Jin
Translated by Nathan K. Mao and Liu Ts'un-yan

《城南舊事》 *Memories of Peking: South Side Stories* (2002)
林海音著　殷張蘭熙、齊邦媛英譯
By Lin Hai-yin
Translated by Nancy C. Ing and Chi Pang-yuan

《阿Q正傳》 *The True Story of Ah Q* (2002)
《祝福及其他》 *The New-Year Sacrifice and Other Stories* (2002)
《野草》 *Wild Grass* (2003)
魯迅著　楊憲益、戴乃迭英譯
By Lu Xun
Translated by Yang Xianyi and Gladys Yang

《臺北人》 *Taipei People* (2000)
白先勇著　白先勇、葉佩霞英譯　喬志高主編
By Pai Hsien-yung
Translated by the Author and Patia Yasin
Edited by George Kao

《沈從文短篇小說選》 *Selected Stories of Shen Congwen* (2004)
沈從文著　金介甫英譯
By Shen Congwen
Translated by Jeffrey C. Kinkley

中國現代文學中英對照系列
Bilingual Series on Modern Chinese Literature

林家鋪子／春蠶
The Shop of the Lin Family
&
Spring Silkworms

中英對照版
Chinese-English Bilingual Edition

茅盾 著
沙博理 英譯

Original Chinese Text by
MAO DUN
Translated by Sidney Shapiro

The Chinese University Press

《林家鋪子/春蠶》(中英對照版)
　　茅盾 著
　　沙博理 英譯

© 香港中文大學 2004 (中〔繁體〕英對照版)

中〔簡體〕英對照版2001年由北京外文出版社出版

國際統一書號 (ISBN) 962–996–045–1

出版：中文大學出版社
　　　香港中文大學 • 香港 新界 沙田
　　　圖文傳真：+852 2603 6692
　　　　　　　　+852 2603 7355
　　　電子郵遞：cup@cuhk.edu.hk
　　　網　　址：www.chineseupress.com

The Shop of the Lin Family & Spring Silkworms
(Chinese-English Bilingual Edition)
　Chinese text by Mao Dun
　Translated by Sidney Shapiro

© **The Chinese University of Hong Kong**, 2004 (Traditional Chinese-English
Bilingual Edition)

Simplified Chinese-English bilingual edition first published in 2001
by Foreign Languages Press, Beijing

ISBN 962–996–045–1

Published by The Chinese University Press,
　The Chinese University of Hong Kong,
　Sha Tin, N.T., Hong Kong.
　Fax: +852 2603 6692
　　　 +852 2603 7355
　E-mail: cup@cuhk.edu.hk
　Web-site: www.chineseupress.com

Printed in Hong Kong

出 版 人 的 話

近二十年，中國與外界接觸日趨頻繁，影響所及，華文作家在世界文學圈中益受注目。二○○○年諾貝爾文學獎由高行健先生獲得，或非偶然。

中文大學出版社一向秉承促進中西方文化交流的使命，故於年前開始籌劃「中國現代文學中英對照系列」，邀得鄭樹森教授出任編輯委員會主席，及幾位國際著名學者出任成員，挑選中國著名作家之重要作品及現有之最佳英譯本，以中英文雙語對照排列出版，計劃每年出書五至六種。個別名作亦會另邀翻譯界高手操刀。各書均邀學界專家特撰新序，以為導讀。

本社謹對編輯委員會及各界友人之鼎力協助，致以熱切謝忱。

Publisher's Note

It is a recent phenomenon that authors of Chinese origin have been attracting more international attention in the literary world, probably as a result of China's increasing cultural interactions with the outside world in the past two decades. As such, it was not coincidental that the 2000 Nobel Prize was awarded to Gao Xingjian, an author of Chinese origin.

With the mission to bridge the gap between Chinese and Western cultures, The Chinese University Press is uniquely situated to play an active role in this area. Thus, this *Bilingual Series on Modern Chinese Literature* has come into existence. Under the able guidance of Professor William Tay and other members of the Advisory Committee, it is planned that five to six titles will be added to the list annually. They will be important works by major authors and will be presented in a bilingual format for cross-cultural appreciation. This means the Committee has either to identify the best existing translations, or to commission experts who can do the job equally well. Each author in the series will also be introduced by a noted scholar in the field to put the work in a critical perspective.

The publisher appreciates the invaluable advice of the Advisory Committee, and sincerely thanks all those who have helped to make this series a reality.

Contents

Introduction by David Der-wei Wang   viii

The Shop of the Lin Family   1

Spring Silkworms   109

目錄

前言 (王德威 撰、湯秋妍 譯)　　　　　　ix

林家鋪子　　　　　　　　　　　　　　1

春蠶　　　　　　　　　　　　　　　109

Introduction*

David Der-wei Wang

Department of East Asian Languages and Cultures
Columbia University, New York

Mao Dun (the pseudonym of Shen Yanbing, 1896–1981), literary critic, novelist, translator, clique-organizer, editor, playwright, essayist, and advocate of Chinese Communism, is one of the most versatile among the May Fourth generation of Chinese literati. As early as the 1920's, Mao Dun systematically introduced western literary ideas and masterpieces into China, with the aim of constructing a new paradigm for modern Chinese fiction. His advocacy and practice of nineteenth-century European naturalism — a branch of realism that highlights hereditary and environmental determinism and "scientific" description — even won him fame as the Chinese spokesman for Zola, father of French naturalism. But just as his pseudonym, Mao Dun (a homonym for contradiction), suggests, his critical and creative works contain many layers of contradiction, calling for continual acts of deciphering by his readers.

Mao Dun started his career as fiction writer in 1927, while he was seeking seclusion after the fiasco of the First Chinese Communist Revolution, which had taken place earlier that year. His first novel *Shi* (Eclipse) deals with young urban leftists' illusion and disillusion during the revolution. It won readers' immediate acclaim for its sympathetic

---

* The introduction is based on chapter 2 of *Fictional Realism in 20th Century China: Mao Dun, Lao She, Shen Congwen* (New York: Columbia University Press, 1992).

前　言

王德威 撰　　　　　　湯秋妍 譯

紐約哥倫比亞大學　　　上海復旦大學

東亞語言與文化系　　　中文系碩士

　　茅盾（本名沈雁冰，1896–1981），身兼文評家、小說家、翻譯家、派系組織家、編輯家、劇作家、散文家、共產主義者等等各種角色，可以說是五四一代文人中最多面的一位。早在1920年代，他就開始有系統地將西方文藝概念與經典作品引介到中國來，希望藉此為中國現代小說建立新的典範。他致力宣導並實踐十九世紀歐洲自然主義 —— 寫實主義文學中強調遺傳和環境決定論以及「科學」描寫的一支，因此贏得了中國左拉（法國自然主義之父）的雅號。然而，誠如他的筆名「茅盾」諧音「矛盾」所暗示的，他的批評及創作文字都包含着多層次的自相矛盾之處，身為讀者必須不斷逐層破解。

　　茅盾於1927年開始他的寫作生涯，時值第一次共產革命失敗的次年，茅盾正在離群索居明哲保身之時。他的第一部小說《蝕》描寫的是革命時期都市左傾青年的夢幻與幻滅。這本書對中產階級革命

treatment of bourgeois revolutionary psychology, its panoramic portraiture of political upheavals in town and country, and its acute presentation of history on the move. Despite this acclaim, the novel also provoked heated debate among critics over such questions as: how can a novelist project reality objectively while adhering to psychological as well as ideological preconceptions? Where are the conceptual and perceptual boundaries of the real for the writer in a given intra- and extra-literary context? and, most poignantly, how should history be represented realistically in fiction?

Eclipse represents only the beginning of Mao Dun's fictional approach to the dynamics of modern Chinese politics and history. His works over a period of two decades chronicle such prominent events as the May Fourth Movement *(Hong* [Rainbow], 1930); *Shuangye hongsi eryuehua* [Maple leaves as red as February flowers], 1943); the May Thirtieth Incident *(Rainbow)*; the Northern Expedition ("Huanmie" [Disillusion], 1930); and the coalition and eventual split between the Chinese Communist Party (CCP) and the left-wing Nationalist party (KMT) government ("Dongyao" [Vacillation], 1930). Mao Dun also wrote about the Nanchang Uprising ("Guling zhiqiu" [Autumn in Guling], 1933); the rise and fall of the First Chinese Communist Revolution ("Zhuiqiu" [Pursuit], 1930); the stormy Shanghai stock market crash *(Ziye* [Midnight], 1933); the Shanghai Resistance of1931 ("Chuncan" [Spring silkworms], 1932); the Second Sino-Japanese War *(Fushi* [Putrefaction], 1941; *Duanlian* [Discipline], 1980); the fall of Hong Kong *Jiehou shiyi* [Pieces picked up after the calamity], 1942); and the New Fourth Army Incident *(Putrefaction,* 1941). Mao Dun's realist fiction is characterized by an urgency to capture what is still fresh in people's memory before it fades away into the realm of the past, as well as by a tendentious motive to defy what has been sanctioned by official historiographers as the orthodox and legitimate. Moreover, given the fact that his works have always been the target of critical

分子的心理作同情的處理、對城鄉政治動盪作宏觀的描述、對變動中的歷史作精確的呈現，這些特點使之立刻獲得讀者的回響。不過，雖然讀者稱譽有加，在評者之間卻引起了熱烈的辯論，重點在：如果一個小說家有心理上以及意識形態上的成見，又怎麼能客觀呈現現實？在特定的文本內外脈絡之下，作家對真實的觀念上與感知上的界線在何處？而最重要的是，小說如何寫實地再現歷史？

《蝕》其實只是茅盾用小說來處理中國現代政治及歷史之變動的開始而已。在四十年之間，他的作品記錄了如五四運動（《虹》，1930；《霜葉紅似二月花》，1943）、五卅案（《虹》）、北伐（《幻滅》，1930）、中國共產黨與國民黨左派的聯盟與最後的決裂（《動搖》，1930）等等重大的事件。茅盾的作品還寫了南昌暴動（《牯嶺之秋》，1933）、第一次共產革命（《追求》，1930）、上海股市崩盤大亂（《子夜》，1933）、1931年的上海抵制事件（《春蠶》，1932）、第二次中日戰爭（《腐蝕》，1941；《鍛煉》，1980）、香港失陷（《劫後拾遺》，1942）、及新四軍事件（《腐蝕》）。茅盾寫實小說的特色就在他急切地捕捉人們記憶猶新、尚未淡入過去世界的事情，他並且還有極具目的性的動機，要抵制官方史學所立為正統、正確的正史。而茅盾的

controversy and censorship, Mao Dun's way of writing about history must itself amount to a political event.

There are two challenges at the core of Mao Dun's fiction. First, his claim to transcribe history faithfully contradicts both the truth claims of official historiography on the one hand and, ironically, the inherent illusoriness of fictional writing itself on the other. Second, his effort to imbue his narrative with a political agenda tempts him to walk the thin line between propaganda and art, between a realism of commitment and a realism of impartiality. History and politics are the two hidden motivations that give rise to Mao Dun's realist novel while threatening to undermine the novel every time it seeks to manifest them. How Mao Dun finds his own realist (dis)course between the Scylla and Charybdis of history and politics, and how he redefines the genres of the historical and the political novel in modern Chinese fiction, are the questions to be explored in the following, and our cases-in-point will be "Spring Silkworms" and "The Shop of the Lin Family." In addition to discussing these two works in their own right, we will also examine their significance in a larger context of other stories and novels Mao Dun wrote at the time.

The early 1930s mark the peak of Mao Dun's career as novelist. Equipped with the two "treasures of naturalism," objective observation and scientific description, as he puts it, Mao Dun conducts his novelistic survey on the changes of China as manifested in both rural and urban areas. For Mao Dun, the early thirties witness the most dramatic moment of China in metamorphosis, a moment whose range of impacts cannot be fully delineated unless one looks at the changes in both town and village, city and country with a simultaneous and organic perspective. Through his surveys and writings, he comes up with a panoramic view of China at the crossroad of contrastive values: agrarian versus industrial models of technology; capitalist versus communist modes of economy; rightist versus leftist leadership;

作品一直都是批評、爭論、文字檢查的焦點，所以他自己寫作歷史
的舉動，本身也就成了一個政治事件。

　　茅盾寫實論述的核心有兩種挑戰。首先，茅盾宣稱要忠實傳鈔
歷史，但是這種宣言卻一方面與官方歷史打對台，一方面又反諷的
與虛構書寫本質上的幻想性質有所衝突。第二，他努力將政治議題
注入他的敘事作品，等於在政治宣傳與藝術、堅持路線的寫實主義
與公正不阿的寫實主義之間的懸空線上起舞。歷史與政治本是茅盾
寫實小說背後的兩大驅動力，然而小說每次試圖彰顯它們，它們反
而擺出鳩佔鵲巢之勢。下文要探討的問題，是茅盾在如危石與渦流
對峙的歷史與政治之間如何找到他自己的寫實論述，以及他如何在
中國現代小說中重新定義歷史小說與政治小說這兩個文類。我們將
着重研究的是《春蠶》與《林家鋪子》。除了討論這兩篇小說本身之
外，我們還將結合茅盾在同時期寫作的其他短篇和長篇小說來探究
它們的意義。

　　1930年代早期正是茅盾小說創作的巔峰期。如他自己所說，挾
「自然主義二寶」之利 —— 客觀觀察與科學描寫，他以小說檢視中國
在鄉間與市鎮所發生的重大變化。對茅盾而言，三十年代初期是中
國蛻變最戲劇性的時刻，其間的衝擊，如非對城鎮與鄉村同時做有
組織的觀察，是不足以深刻描畫的。通過他的檢視與創作，他最後
達成了面臨價值十字路的中國的全面鳥瞰：農業相對於工業技術；
資本主義相對於共產主義經濟模式；右翼相對於左翼領導；衰亡相

decline versus revolution; past versus future. These axes of value do not have to be paralleled in terms of binary opposition; rather each calls for a more careful definition of its own historical rationale. According to Mao Dun's historiographical discourse, there must be some scheme(s) working behind them, linking them in such a way as to bring about the grand schedule of history's unfolding.

Mao Dun's best works in this period, such as the *Nongcun sanbuqu* (Village trilogy) ("Spring Silkworms," "Qiushou" [Autumn harvest], and "Candong" [Winter ruins]), "Linjia puzi" (The shop of the Lin family, 1932), *Duojiao guanxi* (Multifaceted relations, 1936), and *Midnight*, are products of this keen historical concern. Portraying changes and continuities respectively in country, town, and city, these works deserve critical acclaim in their own right. However, one can hardly capture the magnitude of the social/political/economic interactions contained by them till one juxtaposes them and reads them intertextually. Modern Chinese history is so complex for Mao Dun that he has to multiply his narrative sequence in order to chronicle its dynamics in full. It is with this intention, both of offering a simultaneous overview of China at every social stratum and of demonstrating a synchronic version of the diachronic process of time, that Mao Dun proves himself to be one of the most ambitious writers in modem Chinese historical fiction.

The move to "spatialize" history is further reinforced by Mao Dun's effort to expand the range of his subjects. History does not find expression only in revolution, as evinced by his previous works like *Eclipse* and *Rainbow;* rather history has to be substantiated by various social and economic activities, whose mutations point more vividly to the winding course of time and to the inevitable rise of revolution. Thus, Mao Dun constructs a picture of China in the early thirties where at least three time/space junctures or *chronotopes* — rural, urban, and

對於革命；過去相對於未來。這些不同價值所形成的軸線並不一定是以二分相對的方式平行存在的；其實每一種本身都必須以更細緻的方式加以定義其歷史意義。根據茅盾自己的歷史學論述，在這些價值後面必然還有某些計劃在運作，將它們綴合起來，造成歷史的大計劃的逐步實現。

這一時期茅盾最好的作品，像是《農村三部曲》(即《春蠶》、《秋收》、《殘冬》)、《林家鋪子》(1932)、《多角關係》(1936)、及《子夜》，都是他敏銳的歷史關懷下的產物。這些作品描寫鄉間、市鎮、都會中分別發生的變與不變，每部作品本身都具有相當的價值。不過，如果不把這些作品並列來看，彼此參照，就無法捕捉到其中社會/政治/經濟互動關係的廣度。對茅盾來說，中國現代歷史是如此之複雜，若非連續寫作數部小說，不足以完整記錄其發展動態。茅盾既想對中國在每一種社會分層上同時鳥瞰，又要以共時性的版本展現時間的歷史性過程，有此意圖，茅盾才會成為中國現代歷史小說上最具野心的作家之一。

將歷史「空間化」的動作，因茅盾試圖伸展其描寫主題的範圍而更形增強。歷史並非只在革命中才有所表現，茅盾的《蝕》與《虹》對此早已作了見證；其實，歷史表現在各種社會與經濟的活動上，其間的變化更能生動地指出時間委婉的行進與革命的不得不爾。因此，茅盾描畫了三十年代的中國的畫面，在至少三種時間/空間的交

metropolitan — coexist.[1] Each is presided over by figures from different classes: producers, traders, or speculators; and each makes agrarian, entrepreneurial, or speculative activities the dominant sign of its economic and technological system. In my view, *Village Trilogy*, "The Shop of the Lin Family" and *Multifaceted Relations*, and *Midnight* illustrate these three chronotopes.

Mao Dun's purpose is to show that the three most representative social communities are on the verge of breakdown on the eve of a revolution. They threaten each other's existence while they are all well on their own way toward throwing themselves upon the mercy of time. This is the moment when history reaches a finale by gathering all its variegated trajectories onto a single stage. Ideological imperatives notwithstanding, the more interesting issues for the reader are: in what ways Mao Dun conjures up tropes and metaphors to dramatize the coexistence and clash of the three social strata and techno-economical systems; whether he has really carried out his historical vision as he does so; and, even more poignantly, whether his critique of a certain format of historical discourse sometimes betrays a secret endorsement of it. Here, I will concentrate on the first two of the three chronotopes, the rural versus the urban, as demonstrated by *Village Trilogy* and "The Shop of the Lin Family" and *Multifaceted Relations*.

*   *   *

1. "Chronotope" is a term coined by Mikhail Bakhtin. It means a narrative's way of conceptualizing and representing the interrelations of time and space. In the chronotope of literary narratives, according to Bakhtin, "spatial and temporal indicators are fused into one carefully thought-out, concrete whole. Time, as it were, thickens, takes on flesh, becomes artistically visible; likewise, space becomes charged and responsive to the movements of time, plot and history. This intersection of axes and fusion of indicators characterizes the artistic chronotope. … The chronotope as a formally constitutive category determines to a significant degree the image of man in literature as well. The image of man is always intrinsically chronotopic." See Bakhtin, *The Dialogic Imagination*, trans. Caryl Emerson and Michael Holquist (Austin: University of Texas Press, 1981), 84–85.

錯點或者時空輳點 (chronotopes)[1] 上 —— 鄉間、城鎮、都會 —— 同
時並存。這其中的每一種都是由來自各種階級的人物所掌控：生產
者、貿易者、或投機者；每一種都從事農業、企業、或投機的活
動，使其成為經濟與科技系統中的主要表徵。在我看來，《農村三部
曲》、《林家鋪子》和《多角關係》、以及《子夜》分別闡明了這三種時空
輳點。

　　茅盾的目的在於表現最具代表性的三個社會群體都在革命前夕
瀕臨崩潰邊緣。它們威脅彼此的生存，而又紛紛投向時間，任其擺
佈。在這個時刻歷史達到了終場結局，所有不同形貌的彈道航程都
聚集到了同一個舞台上。雖然有意識形態的使命，然而對讀者來說
更有意思的問題是：茅盾如何召遣轉喻與借喻來戲劇化呈現這三種
社會層面與科技/經濟系統之間的並存與衝擊關係；他是否真的實踐
了他的歷史靈視；以及更尖銳的是，他對特定歷史論述的批判，是
否有時反而偷偷泄漏出對它的擁護。在此，我將集中探討這三種時
空輳點中的前兩種，即《農村三部曲》、《林家鋪子》和《多角關係》所
展示的城鎮與鄉村的對立。

＊　　＊　　＊

---

1. 「時空輳點」(chronotope) 一詞出自巴赫汀 (Mikhail Bakhtin)，指的是敘事將時間
與空間之交互關係加以概念化及呈現的方式。根據巴赫汀，在文學性敘事的時空
輳點裡，「空間與時間的指數融為一體，成為細密思維下具體的一個整體。時間
是會凝聚的，會變得有血有肉，在藝術上得以看得出來；相同地，空間也會變得
與時間、情節、與歷史的運動相呼應。這個軸線的交錯與指數的融合就是藝術上
時空輳點的特徵……時空輳點作為一個形式上的組成範疇，在相當重要的程度上
也決定了文學中人的形象。人的形象在內涵上其實永遠都是一種時空輳點。」見
Bakhtin, *The Dialogic Imagination*, trans. Caryl Emerson and Michael Holquist
(Austin: University of Texas, 1981), 84–85。

Mao Dun's *Village Trilogy* is a sensitive portrayal of Chinese peasants experiencing the economic and political storms of the thirties. "Spring Silkworms," the first story in the trilogy, has been especially praised for its compelling exposé of the declining agrarian mode of production in the countryside vis-à-vis the rise of modern technology and speculative investment in the city. Written at the same time as another much bigger project, *Midnight*, the novel of aggressive capitalism set in Shanghai, "Spring Silkworms" represents a part of Mao Dun's historical dialectic that highlights the confrontation of modern machinery with provincial handicraftsmanship; of western know-how with native values; and of a capitalist monopoly with the rural struggle for cultural and socioeconomic autonomy. Mao Dun intends an account that would favor neither side, since to him real history manifests its meaning only amid a pre-revolutionary setting. Contradictions and conflicts are what he aims to describe; there are moments, however, when fewer contradictions surge up than expected, and when conflicts take place out of their set context. This exposes the gaps in his historical discourse and its privileging of an external position.

The question at the center of "Spring Silkworms" is the future of Chinese textile technology; the story raises the issue of a changing work ethic, a concept of management, a marketing strategy, and even a locale for those who are involved in this technology's various stages of practice. In "Spring Silkworms," through the tale of the old farmer, Lao Tongbao, and his family's bitter experience with raising silkworms, Mao Dun brings to light not just the procedures of the traditional form of sericulture but also its socio-psychological impact. The peasants take care of the silkworms with a religious fervor otherwise reserved for ritual. From speaking to eating, every facet of life must be devoted to the nurture of silkworms; every taboo must be cautiously avoided. During the incubation period, husbands are even forbidden to sleep

　　茅盾的《農村三部曲》是對中國農民在三十年代經歷經濟與政治風暴的敏銳描畫。《春蠶》是三部曲的第一個故事，對農業生產模式面對現代科技興起與城市投機投資時的衰敗過程有極動人的揭露，向為評者所稱譽。《春蠶》的寫作時間約與茅盾另一個大型的寫作計劃，即描寫上海資本主義的《子夜》同時，而《春蠶》代表的是茅盾歷史辯證的一部分，處理現代機械文明與地方手工業的衝突；西方知識與本土價值觀的衝突；資本主義獨霸與鄉村爭取文化與社經自主權的衝突。茅盾想要做的記錄是不偏袒任何一方，因為對他來說，歷史惟有在革命前的場景中才能展現其意義。衝突與摩擦就是他想要描寫的；然而，也有某些時刻，衝突不若預期中來得多，而摩擦又在非預期的情況下發生。這一點揭露了他歷史論述中的縫隙，以及其對外在地位的偏愛。

　　《春蠶》的中心問題是中國織造技術的未來；故事提出變化中的工作倫理，管理的觀念，市場的策略，甚至還涉入這個科技實踐之各個階段的人們的所在場所。透過《春蠶》中老農夫老通寶的故事，以及他的家人養蠶的艱辛經驗，茅盾所揭露的不只是傳統養蠶業的工作流程，更是其中社會心理的衝擊。農人從事養蠶的態度，一如虔誠地進行宗教儀式。從說話到吃飯，生命中任何一部分都必須投注於養蠶；養蠶業中每一個禁忌都必須嚴格規避。在孵化期，

with their wives, who hatch the eggs of the silkworms in their bosoms. The critic C. T. Hsia points out the humanitarian ethos underlying the story: "Although it is [Mao Dun's] articulate intention to discredit this kind of feudal mentality, his loving portrayal of good peasants at their customary tasks transforms the supposed Communist tract into a testament of humanity."[2]

As a result of their hard labor, the peasants reap an abundant crop of cocoons. But the harvest soon turns out to be a disaster; most silk factories have shut down as a consequence of the armed conflict between the Chinese and Japanese in the Shanghai area, and there is no need for cocoons. Lao Tongbao's family is forced to sell their crop at a great loss and falls deeper in debt than ever for all their season's hard work and worries. The same ironic disaster of over-production happens in "Autumn Harvest," part two of Mao Dun's trilogy. Lao Tongbao and his family try their luck in growing rice but, once again, the more they harvest, the more they lose. By the end of the story, Lao Tongbao, dying in bed, finally concedes to his rebellious son, A Duo, that there is something else working upon man's fate: "How come you should prove to be the right one? How strange it is!"[3]

Notice how the naturalist treasures of scientific observation and objective description work here to transmit an unprecedentedly close look at the process of sericulture. Mao Dun may not necessarily be an expert on the silkworm raising industry, but by detailing a farm family's hardships in the new naturalist-scientific way, he manages to usher his readers into a world where the diseased mode of production is still under way, even though history has evolved to the next stage

---

2. C. T. Hisa, *A History of Modern Chinese Fiction* (New Haven: Yale University Press, 1961), 163.
3. Mao Dun, "Qiushou" (Autumn harvest), *Mao Dun quanji* (Complete works of Mao Dun) (Beijing: Renmin wenxue chubanshe, 1985), 8:368.

夫妻甚至不可同房，因為妻子是在自己的胸腔上孵蠶卵的。夏志清曾指出這個故事中的人道主義精神：「雖然茅盾刻意要顯示這種封建精神的不足之處，然而他心存關愛地描畫依照習俗工作的善良農民，卻把原先應該是共產主義的文字轉化成一個人性的約囑。」[2]

在一番辛苦之後，農人採收到大批的蠶繭。然而豐收很快就變成災難；多半的絲廠都已經因為上海地區中日雙方的軍事衝突而關閉，不再需要蠶繭了。老通寶一家被迫降價求售，虧了大本，一場辛苦反而使他們陷入前所未有的債務裏。在茅盾三部曲的第二部《秋收》裏，也發生了同樣反諷的過度生產的災難。老通寶一家這次嘗試種稻，但是悲劇重演，收穫越多，損失越大。到了故事結束時，易簀之際的老通寶終於向他叛逆的兒子多多頭讓步，承認人的命運非由自主：「真想不到你是對的！真奇怪！」[3]

我們注意到科學觀察與客觀描述這所謂自然主義之寶如何在此傳達出對養蠶業前所未見的細密觀察。茅盾或許並非養蠶專家，但是他以自然主義/科學方式細節處理農家的辛勞，的確把讀者擁入一個雖然歷史早已走入下一個階段，而過時的生產方式仍在進行的世

---

2. C. T. Hsia, *A History of Modern Chinese Fiction* (New Haven: Yale University Press, 1961), 163.

3. 茅盾：《秋收》，《茅盾全集》(北京：人民文學出版社，1985)，8:368。

of its set course. Without the practice of a new narrative discourse, the old silkworm raising business would not have been so conspicuously scrutinized by writers who behave like scientists, nor would it have set itself off so poignantly as something disappearingly quaint for the delectation of enlightened readers. Mao Dun thus makes himself at least sound more persuasive than traditional storytellers when he describes the recession of the old technology as a stage of Chinese history, generating a new rhetorical power in his seemingly neutral discourse.

Nevertheless, Mao Dun's scientific accounts carry gaps and inconsistencies, pointing to a deep-lying dispute within both his narrative and his ideological discourses. In order to accentuate the vulnerability of the traditional silk industry in a time of rapid political and economic changes, Mao Dun is committed to adding more and more blows to the family of Lao Tongbao. In so doing, he reveals his predilection for melodramatic arrangement in the name of naturalist experimentalism, with the visible difference that a Chinese version of communism has been brought in to substitute for the old Darwinian positivist hypotheses. Before things get better as a result of revolution, they will first have to get worse in every perceivable way. The deterministic elements of Zolaesque theory are again neatly reinterpreted by Mao Dun as a heritage of feudalistic consciousness and an environment of pre-capitalist society, which predetermine the Chinese peasantry's fate; the old concept of the Wheel of Fortune cycles through another turn.

The problem goes deeper. A well-known leftist writer, Mao Dun is theoretically writing to document the downfall of traditional rural technology on the eve of the impending capitalist monopoly of China's economy and industry. But, as has been pointed out by critics, he describes the peasants' hard work and unfaltering trust in Deity with such an understanding tone that the story comes out more as a

界中。如果沒有這新式的敘事論述，舊式的養蠶業就不會受到像科學家一樣的作家如此細膩的處理，也不會為了滿足啟蒙讀者之故，將自身設定成一個消失中的奇景。因此，茅盾在描寫作為中國歷史階段之一的舊科技之落伍時，至少比傳統說書人要具有說服力得多，在他看似中立的論述中發出了新的修辭力量。

然而，茅盾的科學式記錄有許多縫隙，指出了他的敘事與意識形態論述之間潛藏的爭論。為了突顯政治與經濟劇變時代中傳統養蠶業的軟弱無助，茅盾立意一次又一次地打擊老通寶一家。而這麼做，適足以泄漏他雖然以自然主義實驗為名，其實卻偏好煽情悲喜劇的情節安排，最明顯的不同在於中國式的共產主義被引入來取代舊的達爾文式的實證假設。在天下事可以因革命而改善以前，必須先在各方面都惡化到極點才行。茅盾又一次將左拉式的決定論因數重新詮釋成一個封建意識的傳承以及前資本主義社會的環境，就是這些決定了中國農民的命運；舊式的命運之輪的觀念又輪轉了一圈。

而問題還要更進一層。茅盾身為知名左翼作家，理論上他的寫作應該記錄傳統鄉村技術在資本主義壟斷中國經濟與工業之前夕的沈淪。但是，正如批評家早已指出的，他描述農民的辛勤工作與以及對神明不動搖的信心，其口氣之同情了解，使得這個故事成為對

celebration of their endurance and patience than as a critique of their superstition and conservatism. Even the title of the story, "Spring Silkworms," suggests an overtone of romantic melancholy, with its allusion to the famous lines from the Tang poet Li Shangyin's poem "Wuti" (Untitled):

> And the silkworms of spring will weave until they die
> And every night the candles will weep their wicks away.[4]

Lao Tongbao serves as the spokesman for values which are admittedly out of date, but judged by his family's current predicament, one wonders if the superstitions of the past may not have been better comfort than the promises of the present. Has Mao Dun unintentionally revealed a reactionary consciousness? Or, more equivocally, has he suspended ideological and moral judgment, and made his text a space of uncertainties?

It is due to this ironic narrative potential that the story enhances rather than settles the tension that arises between old and new concepts of technology at a historical juncture. Mao Dun's political point of view leads him to see history as a progressive evolution toward a communist millennium — thus the stage of rural manual labor has to yield to that of capitalist investment and mass production — as reflected exactly by *Midnight*. Yet one discerns from this formula the bothersome paradox that, before the final revolution comes, history manifests a regressive development, with each new stage of social structure (and mode of production) being one degree inferior to the previous one. If, as critics have pointed out, the Marxist scheme reenacts the plot of the fortunate fall of Christianity, in which paradise is lost in order to be regained, and in which each age is more sinful and miserable than the

---

4. Li Shangyin, "Wuti," in *Jade Mountain*, trans. Witter Bynner (New York: Knoft, 1957), 81.

農民的耐力與耐心的歌頌，而不再是對他們的迷信與保守的批判了。甚至故事的題目《春蠶》都有一種浪漫傷感的暗示，遠溯唐代李商隱《無題》詩中的名句：

春蠶到死絲方盡　　蠟炬成灰淚始乾[4]

老通寶是過時價值體系的代言人，然而由他的家庭所面臨的困境看來，我們不禁懷疑，或者昔日的迷信還比現在的承諾來得令人心安。茅盾是否無意間泄漏了反動的意識？或者更模稜兩可的，他是否懸置了意識形態與道德判斷，而使得他的作品成為一個充滿不確定的空間？

正因為有這種反諷的敘事潛力，所以故事事實上是加強而非安撫在歷史交界處新與舊的科技觀念之間的緊張關係。茅盾的政治觀點使他將歷史看成一個朝向共產主義太平盛世而前進的進化過程——因此農村的人工勞力必然要向資本主義投資與大量生產低頭讓位，正如《子夜》一書所反映的。然而我們從這個公式裏看到了一個令人困擾的弔詭，就是說，在最後革命到來之前，歷史表現出來的是一種倒退的發展，每一個新的社會結構的階段（以及生產方式）較諸前一階段都要退步一截。如果，如批評家所指出的，馬克思主義的設計重演了基督教幸運墮落的情節，也就是說樂園之所以失落乃是為了復得，而每一個時代都要比前一個更罪惡、更可憐，這樣才

---

4. 李商隱：《無題》，*Jade Mountain*, trans. Witter Bynner (New York: Knoft, 1957), 81.

last, in preparation for the Millennium,[5] then Mao Dun's interpretation of Marxism is further bolstered by a Chinese concept of the cyclical mechanism of history. Revolutionary anticipation and reactionary nostalgia thus coalesce, reflecting a simultaneous affirmation of inevitable progress and increasing alienation; one in which progress is only apparent because of one's awareness of ultimate salvation, not from any contemporary evidence.

The two parts of the trilogy, "Autumn Harvest" and "Winter Ruins," present farmers simply trapped deeper by the gratuitousness of their labor. Before his younger son A Duo's revolutionary consciousness is acted upon, Lao Tongbao and his family are living in an increasingly worsening condition; for this reason, Lao Tongbao's nostalgia for the arguable "good old days" is not absolutely blameworthy. Situated in such a self-contradictory vision of historical movement, Mao Dun's nostalgic record of the old customs of silkworm raising is not necessarily a sign of his latent reactionary consciousness; rather, it could serve as an indicator, hinting at his foreknowledge of how the forthcoming capitalist age would be even less rational and human in both economic and moral terms. In a way unexpected by Mao Dun and orthodox leftist critics, this inconsistency in reasoning reinforces the drama of the trilogy while posing a more serious question: has Mao Dun's wholesale introduction of new narrative and economic/historical models also paved the way for a new mythology?

The peasants' burgeoning desire for revolt and revolution provides the major motivation of the trilogy. Contrasted with it, nevertheless, is a less noticeable (but just as powerful) yearning for the return of the mythic Order of Heaven. Mao Dun makes it clear that the former is

---

5. See, for example, Dominick LaCapra, *Soundings in Critical Theory* (Ithaca: Cornell University Press, 1989), 155–181.

能為最後太平做準備，[5] 那麼支撐茅盾對馬克思主義重新詮釋的，其實更是一個中國式視歷史為迴圈運轉的觀念。革命的預期及反動的懷鄉情愁於焉合併，同時認可了不可避免的進步與不斷滋長的疏離；在這種認可中，因為對最終救贖有所自覺，進步才能顯而易見，這不是從任何當代的證據中看得出來的。

三部曲的後兩部《秋收》與《殘冬》呈現出農民因勞動得不到報償而陷得更深的情況。在小兒子多多頭的革命意識尚未作用前，老通寶一家的情況可謂每下愈況；因此，老通寶緬懷往日的好時光，倒也情有可原。身處對歷史活動如此自我矛盾的視野中，茅盾對舊日養蠶業習俗懷舊式的記錄倒不見得是他潛藏的反動意識的表徵，反倒是一種指標，暗指他認識到未來資本主義時代在經濟與道德層面都將比較不理性與不人性。以茅盾本人及正統左翼批評家未曾預料到的方式，這個推理上的前後矛盾反而強化了三部曲的戲劇性，而同時又提出了一個更嚴肅的問題：茅盾對新的敘事與經濟/歷史模式的全面引介，是否也為一個新的神話鋪好了路？

農民對反抗與革命逐漸萌發的欲望是三部曲中最主要的動力。而與此相對的，還有對回歸神秘天道秩序的一種雖較不明顯但同樣重要的渴求。茅盾說得很清楚，前者是植基於人類的意願的，而後

---

5. 例如，Dominick LaCapra, *Soundings in Critical Theory* (Ithaca: Cornell University Press, 1989), 155–181。

based on human will and volition while the latter derives its power from nothing but passive superstitions about heavenly grace. Ideally, we are supposed to witness the two contrasting forces crossing each other somewhere in the trilogy — the death of Lao Tongbao, for instance, or the peasants' robbery of local rich men's barns — with one incident losing its mysterious spell and the other winning more and more recognition. But the way Mao Dun writes about these forces solicits a different reading. Throughout the trilogy, the two forces never really exchange positions but, rather, parallel each other, gaining more strength. One still remembers how the prophet like Taoist monk, Huang, spreads rumors about oracular signs and omens and gathers more and more followers, as A Duo and other young farmers organize themselves to stir up troubles against the rich and powerful. By the end of "Winter Ruins," A Duo and his fellow rebels finally rise against the local authorities, amid rumors of the descent of the new Heavenly Prince.

In this sense, the ending of the trilogy is highly ambiguous. The allegedly descended Heavenly Prince, a poor, naive kid, is arrested by nervous, local armed forces. It is A Duo who unexpectedly comes to his rescue while attacking the prison. Laughing at his discovery of the identity of the "Heavenly Prince," A Duo sends him away and thus reaffirms his own cause. This rescue emblemizes less a cancellation than a replacement of the mythical heavenly mandate. The confrontation between the leader of farm insurgents and the chosen candidate for heaven's will leads the reader to wonder if they share any common ground in reflecting the utopian wish of the Chinese peasantry. According to Mao Dun's plan, the climax of his *Village Trilogy* portrays a progression of history towards the goal of Revolution. Given the novel's hidden yearning for a regressive mode of rescue from time, however, one may take one step further and say the linear development in either progressive or regressive form is only part of a cycle, an

者的力量則恰恰來自對天賜恩惠的被動式迷信。理想上，我們應當
會看到這兩種相反的力量在三部曲的某一部份彼此交錯 —— 例如老
通寶之死，或是農民搶劫當地富人的穀倉的一幕 —— 而其中之一將
失去其神秘的力量，另一個則獲得愈來愈多的認可。然而，茅盾描
寫這些力量的方式卻引起一種全然不同的閱讀。三部曲通篇，這兩
種力量其實從未交換地位，而是彼此平行，而且都更增強了。我們
猶然記得先知形象的黃道士到處散播有關異象的謠言，藉此吸引更
多的追隨者，而同時多多頭與其他年輕的農民正組織起來與有錢有
勢者作對。《殘冬》的結尾，多多頭與其它的反抗分子終於公開與地
方勢力對抗，而其時新的真命天子臨凡的謠言卻也正甚囂塵上。

在這個場面中，三部曲的結局可謂曖昧至極。所謂的真命天子
臨凡，是一個窮苦人家的天真男孩，他被緊張的地方武力所逮捕。
而解救他的，竟是前來攻打監獄的多多頭。多多頭發現所謂真命天
子的真實身份，不覺啞然失笑，隨便把他打發走了，也更加堅定自
己的信念。然而，這場解救所象徵的，不是神秘天命的消解，反倒
是取代。農民叛變的領袖與天命所擇的聖主之間的衝突，令讀者不
禁懷疑他們是否都反映着中國農民的烏托邦願望。根據茅盾的計
劃，《農村三部曲》的高潮將描繪歷史朝革命目標邁進的歷程。然而
作品其實隱藏着對從時間獲得解救的後退模式的渴望，所以我們不
妨更進一步地說，不論前進或後退的直線發展，其實都只是迴圈的

alternation of chaos and order underlined by the periodic return of revolution. Last but not least, Mao Dun intends to write an initiation story about Chinese peasants' voluntary fight against the powers of Nature and Heaven, but just as the titles of his three stories indicate, the mythical rhythm formed by the cycle of seasons is only too well reestablished at the level of discourse.

*   *   *

After *Village Trilogy,* Mao Dun's geo-historical itinerary leads next to the towns and small cities, intermediary areas linking the countryside, where Lao Tongbao and his family take up residence, and to metropolitan Shanghai, where capitalist tycoons and investors thrive. These towns form a second chronotope, a temporal/spatial context that regulates human relations less in terms of labor than in terms of commercial transaction. The change of the chronotopic mode must affect the representational system that makes reality what it is. Instead of farmers, small shop proprietors and provincial enterprise owners constitute the prominent class of this society. Money, rather than commodity, is the new metaphor that gives meaning to the society under discussion.

One can hardly forget the long list of Tang Zijia's bank accounts, loans, mortgages, rent incomes, pawnshop earnings, uncashed checks, houses, realty investments, land, and other valuables that appears at the very beginning of the novel *Multifaceted Relations;* or the meticulous reports of the financial fluctuations of Mr. Lin's grocery store throughout the story of "The Shop of the Lin Family." Indeed, Tang Zijia and Mr. Lin represent two stereotypes in Mao Dun's gallery of small-town figures. Tang Zijia is a landlord now turned into a modern entrepreneur. He lives by collecting rent from his tenants, and running a pawnshop and a silk factory. Mr. Lin, on the other hand, manages a grocery store, which is also a private credit union for lower-class

一部分，乃是由按時回潮的革命所裝點的混沌與秩序的轉換。最後，茅盾意圖寫作一個關於中國農民自發性地與大自然與老天爺抗爭的啟蒙故事，然而正如這三個故事的題目所指出的，季節迴圈所形成的神秘節奏其實是只在論述的層面上才能重建起來的。

＊　　＊　　＊

在《農村三部曲》之後，茅盾的土地歷史式行程的下一站就是鄉鎮與小城了，也就是連接老通寶一家安身立命的鄉村與資本主義大戶揚名立萬的大都會上海的仲介地帶。這些城鎮形成第二種時空輳點，一個時間上／空間上的脈絡，以商業行為而非勞力來規範人際關係。時空輳點模式的轉變必然影響到使現實所以為現實的再現系統。在這裏農民不再是主角，小商家與地方企業主才是這個社會的主要階層。金錢，而非商品，才是賦予這個社會意義的新暗喻。

任誰也難忘《多角關係》一開頭唐子嘉一長串的銀行戶頭、放款、貸款、租金收入、當鋪盈餘、待兌支票、房產、不動產投資、土地、以及其他的財產；或者《林家鋪子》這篇故事中，林先生雜貨店之財務變動的精細無比的報表。的確，唐子嘉跟林先生代表了茅盾小城人物大觀中的兩種典型。唐子嘉是由地主轉成的現代企業家。他向租戶收租，並經營當鋪跟絲廠。而林先生則開設雜貨店，也同時為低階層的人們提供私人的借帳服務。茅盾以標準巴爾扎克

people. In a strictly Balzac-like manner, Mao Dun depicts these two characters' business activities as if they were indices to a monstrous mechanism from which nobody can escape. *Midnight,* it will be recalled, also deals with the power of money. Whereas to characters in "The Shop of the Lin Family" and *Multifaceted Relations* money means more or less a contractual emblem for goods, thereby taking on a certain material value, money exposes its abstract nature in the hands of the tycoons, stockbrokers, and speculators in *Midnight,* proliferating or diminishing in such a relentless fashion as to threaten the whole sign system of commerce. The conception of money, therefore, is endowed with a new moral exchange-value at each stage of economic/historical development.

The three enterprises run by Tang Zijia in *Multifaceted Relations,* land, pawnshop, and factory, neatly form a web that capture most farmers like Lao Tongbao and his family. Tang Zijia rents his land and structures on the ground to tenants, reinvesting his rent income in factories that make products far beyond the farmers' ability to acquire. To ease the financial stringency of the poor, his pawnshop is always ready to buy things for a price much lower than their true value. Linked together, the three enterprises supplement each other's needs, thus enabling Tang Zijia to accumulate fortunes indefinitely, as time surges forward in its linear fashion.

But the novel is not about how well things are going for the landlord entrepreneur. Instead, it tells a story of the way the machine of fortune runs out of gear at a time full of unpredictable economic and political upheavals. As early as chapter three, we are informed that Tang's pawnshop has gone bankrupt, followed by the news that his clerks are having trouble collecting rents in the countryside. Worse, the workers of his silk factory are about to launch a strike in protest against unpaid work. Throughout the novel, Tang Zijia runs around to find support to fill in his financial holes, but his banker friends all

的方式描寫這兩個人物的生意，好象無人能脫逃的惡魔般的大機制的指標。我們馬上會看見，《子夜》也同樣處理金錢的力量的問題。而對《林家舖子》及《多角關係》中的人物來說，金錢多少意味着貨品的契約性象徵，所以帶有某種物質的價值，而在《子夜》中，在大亨、證券業者、以及投機分子的手上，金錢的抽象本質被揭露了，其孳生或縮減是絕對不講人情的，直可威脅到整個商業的象徵系統。因此，金錢的概念如今在每一個經濟／歷史發展的階段，都有一個新的道德的交換價值。

《多角關係》中唐子嘉所經營的三種企業 —— 土地、當舖、工廠 —— 形成了一張密實的網，足以罩住所有像老通寶一家這樣的農民。唐子嘉將他的土地跟地上物出租，又將所得的租金再投資到工廠上，而生產出的商品遠遠超過農民的負擔能力。而為了紓解窮人財務上的困窘，他的當舖又以逸待勞，以遠低於其真正價值的價錢買進物品。這三種企業連合起來，互相補足，使唐子嘉的財富在時間直線發展的過程中無盡地累積。

不過，小說倒並不是寫地主企業家一路發的故事。反之，故事講的是在充滿不可預測的經濟與政治動亂的時代中，幸運之輪隨時可能脫軌。早在第三章，我們就知道唐家的當舖破產了，繼之他家的夥計在鄉下又收不到租。更糟的是，絲廠的工人正準備發動罷工，抗議僱主拖欠薪資。整部小說中，唐子嘉都在四處跑頭寸，挖東補西，而他在銀行界的朋友卻一概拒絕他的請托，害怕承擔風險。然而，此處所牽涉的問題在於唐子嘉跟他財務情況較好的朋友

turn him down simply through fear of high risk. The problem involved here, nevertheless, is that Tang Zijia is as much a loser as his financier friends. If Tang suffers from an overstock of goods in his factory, his friends suffer from an overstock of money in their safes. Just as he sighs at the end of the novel, "This is really a bizarre year! So many stores and factories are paralyzed because of running out of reserves; but the financial business is paralyzed, too, only because of keeping too much money out of circulation — it is going to be stifled to death."[6]

A similar problem happens to Mr. Lin in "The Shop of the Lin Family," though both his fortune and business are much smaller in scale than Tang Zijia's. A tailor-made character representing the petit bourgeois class in China, Mr. Lin runs his grocery store in an old fashioned way. He buys things cheap in large quantity and sells them at a higher price to his customers, while at the same time he absorbs their extra money and runs it like a private credit union. According to Mao Dun's moral standard, Mr. Lin may not always be an honest merchant, since he makes money by taking advantage of buyers and creditors, but he is otherwise a good person among family members and friends. This makes him a much more complicated character than Tang Zijia, especially when he is faced with the fate of impending bankruptcy. Mr. Lin has no intention of failing the clients of his small credit union, but, when customers cannot afford to buy his goods and business runs more and more slowly, he finds himself unable to live up to his reputation as a trustworthy man.

From the viewpoint of vulgar communism, one may easily conclude that neither Tang Zijia nor Mr. Lin deserves sympathy, because they are exploiters of the majority, as in the case of the family

---

6. Mao Dun, *Duojiao guanxi* (Multifaceted relations), *Mao Dun quanji*, 4:114.

其實根本都是同樣的大輸家。若說唐子嘉的問題是工廠裏囤積了過多的貨品，則他的朋友們則苦於保險櫃裏存了過多的金錢。正如他在小說結尾感歎的：「這年頭兒真古怪！有多少『事業』，——多少商家廠家周轉不來，僵在那裏；然而銀錢業也說他們有多少現款活動不來，也是僵在那裏，——他們是要脹死！」[6]

《林家鋪子》中的林先生也有類似的遭遇，雖然他的財富事業比起唐子嘉來可謂小巫見大巫。林先生是量身訂做出來的中國小布爾喬亞階級代表人物，他的雜貨店完全以古法經營。他以低價大量買進，以高價賣出，再以他吸收的剩餘資金開設私人銀行。根據茅盾的道德標準，林先生取利於買主與借貸人，雖未必稱得上誠實公道，但是就家人與朋友來說，卻是個不折不扣的好人。就這一點來說他比唐子嘉要複雜得多，尤其是當他面臨破產的命運時。林先生無意欺騙他的私人銀行的客戶，但是當客人買不起他的貨品，生意愈來愈清淡，他也就當不成一個誠實可靠的人了。

由粗糙共產主義的觀點來看，結論很容易，那就是唐子嘉跟林先生都不值得同情，因為他們剝削像老通寶一家那樣的大眾。不過

---

6. 茅盾：《多角關係》，《茅盾全集》，4:114。

of Lao Tongbao. But Mao Dun has something else to say about their downfall. He sees in it a signal through which the forces of time and history are made themselves intelligible to people living amid them. In the *Village Trilogy*, as we remember, not until the final moment of the farmers' insurgence is time passively felt by them in terms of the cycle of nature and of the Wheel of Fortune. In the cases of both Tang Zijia and Mr. Lin, however, time is a much more active element. Timing, on top of time, is the key factor determining their gains or loses. They see the right moment to buy and sell commodities, and they reinvest their earnings at a time most favorable to their interest. News and rumors about political or economic jolts happening far away in Shanghai have a significant effect on their businesses. Time and timing correspond to each other but do not necessarily form a causal relation. Bad times such as war, famine, or flood may actually provide a good chance for a Mr. Lin or Tang Zijia to make money — particularly if they time every move shrewdly.

Insofar as Tang Zijia and Mr. Lin recognize the irreversible passage of time and consciously make the best use of every fleeting moment, history demonstrates itself in "The Shop of the Lin Family" and *Multifaceted Relations* more as a linear flux of forces involving visible signs of human awareness and effort than in *Village Trilogy*. The question posited by Mao Dun, nevertheless, is why, given all their perception of time and timing, both Tang Zijia and Mr. Lin fail so disastrously. History seems to contain a sly power that outwits even those who are on full alert. One can certainly find easy explanations on the surface of Mao Dun's narrative account. Cheap foreign goods, especially things made in Japan, are said to be the major evil cause of disturbance in the otherwise stable Chinese market. But just as the center part of "The Shop of the Lin Family" demonstrates, even if Mr. Lin and his competitors sell Japanese products, despite the students' nationalist campaign against them, they find themselves still losing

對這兩人的沒落，茅盾另有話說。他在其中看到了一個信號，時間與歷史將自己的力量展現給人知道的信號。我們還記得在《農村三部曲》中，直到農民揭竿而起的最後一刻，時間才被動地以自然的迴圈與命運巨輪的形象為人們所感知。然而在唐子嘉與林先生的例子裏，時間的角色卻主動多了。時機取代了單純的時間，成為決定他們成敗的關鍵因素。他們看出最佳時機去買進及賣出，又在最有利的時機將所得的利潤重新投資。八百里遠的政治或經濟變動的消息與謠言在上海都對他們的生意有着重大影響。時間與時機彼此照應，但卻未必形成因果關係。像戰爭、饑荒、洪水這類的壞時間，卻可能為林先生或唐子嘉這樣的人提供賺錢的大好時機 —— 尤其是如果他們精明地在最佳時間採取行動的話。

如果說唐子嘉跟林先生認識到時間不可逆向的流動，並且善加利用每一個飛逝的時刻，則《林家鋪子》與《多角關係》中展現出來的歷史，較之《農村三部曲》，就更是牽涉到人類自覺與自力之可見徵象的一股直線進行的流動力量了。然而，茅盾所提出的問題是，既然唐子嘉與林先生如此通曉時間與時機的道理，為什麼他們還是落得個悲慘的結局呢？歷史似乎有一股莫可名狀的狡詐力量，足以智取最警覺的人。我們當然很容易在茅盾敘事的表面上找到解釋。便宜的舶來品，尤其是日貨，一般相信正是在原本穩定的中國市場上造成騷動的首惡。但是正如《林家鋪子》的中段部分所顯示的，雖然林先生跟他的競爭者不顧學生國族主義的抗議，都開始賣日貨，但

money. There must be some element yet unperceivable to Mao Dun's businessman characters, turning them from victimizers into the victims of their time.

Besides money, a correlated emblem of the ongoing commercial activities is the credit contract. Contracts are regulative mechanisms designed to guarantee the terms of an exchange between individuals in a set temporal context. For investors, credit contracts promise a return of their capital plus interest by the end of the stated amount of time. In "The Shop of the Lin Family" and *Multifaceted Relations*, when money is running short, credit contracts are in immediate jeopardy, too. Since Mr. Lin's personal credit union is nurtured especially on the savings of low-income people, the bankruptcy of his store brings about pathetic family tragedies.

"The Shop of the Lin Family" ends with a widow going insane after she loses all her life savings. Whereas man's contract with Heaven is already broken, as shown by works such as *Village Trilogy*, men's contracts among themselves are still doomed to fail. It is here that Mao Dun reasserts the ironic moral conclusion he has reached in *Village Trilogy*: time betrays, both in the sense that it fails people's trust in their fate or future, and in the sense that it reveals the falsity of such a trust. But the story is not yet over. *Midnight* is the next chapter in Mao Dun's grand narrative of time and history.

還是不斷賠錢蝕本。此中必然有些因素是茅盾筆下的生意人角色尚無法了解的，以致他們最後都從加害者變成了時代的受害者。

除了金錢，不斷進行的各種商業活動的一個共同表徵是信用契約。契約是規範性的運作規則，用以保證某特定時間內個人之間交換活動的條件。對投資者來說，信用契約代表着在契約聲明的時間到期後，他們拿回的是連本帶利。在《林家鋪子》與《多角關係》中，當現錢不夠了，信用契約也就馬上陷入危機。因為林先生私人銀行的主要客戶是低收入者，所以他的店子破產就帶來了可悲可歎的家庭悲劇。

《林家鋪子》的結尾描寫一個寡婦在失去畢生積蓄後發瘋的景象。人類與老天的契約早已打破，正如《農村三部曲》所表現的，而人與人之間的契約又同樣注定要灰飛煙滅。茅盾就是在此處再一次肯定他在《農村三部曲》所達到的反諷道德結論：時間會背叛，它讓人們對自己命運或未來的信心破產，也揭露出這種信心的虛偽。但是故事還沒完。《子夜》將揭開茅盾時間與歷史的宏大敘事的下一篇章。

林家鋪子

The Shop of the Lin Family

The Shop of the Lin Family

I

Miss Lin's small mouth was pouting when she returned home from school that day. She flung down her books, and instead of combing her hair and powdering her nose before the mirror as usual, she stretched out on the bed. Her eyes staring at the top of the bed canopy, Miss Lin lay lost in thought. Her little cat leaped up beside her, snuggled against her waist and miaowed twice. Automatically, she patted his head, then rolled over and buried her face in the pillow.

"Ma!" called Miss Lin.

No answer. Ma, whose room was right next door, ordinarily doted on this only daughter of hers. On hearing her return, Ma would come swaying in to ask whether she was hungry. Ma would be keeping something good for her. Or she might send the maid out to buy a bowl of hot soup with meat dumplings from a street vendor.... But today was odd. There obviously were people talking in Ma's room — Miss Lin could hear Ma hiccuping too — yet Ma didn't even reply.

Again Miss Lin rolled over on the bed, and raised her head. She would eavesdrop on this conversation. Whom could Ma be talking to, that voices had to be kept so low?

But she couldn't make out what they were saying. Only Ma's continuous hiccups wafted intermittently to Miss Lin's ears. Suddenly,

林家鋪子

林小姐這天從學校回來就撅起着小嘴唇。她摜下了書包，並不照例到鏡台前梳頭髮搽粉，卻倒在牀上看着帳頂出神。小花噗的也跳上牀來，挨着林小姐的腰部摩擦，咪嗚咪嗚地叫了兩聲。林小姐本能地伸手到小花頭上摸了一下，隨即翻一個身，把臉埋在枕頭裏，就叫道：

「媽呀！」

沒有回答。媽的房就在間壁，媽素常疼愛這唯一的女兒，聽得女兒回來就要搖搖擺擺走過來問她肚子餓不餓，媽留着好東西呢，——再不然，就差吳媽趕快去買一碗餛飩。但今天卻作怪，媽的房裏明明有說話的聲音，並且還聽得媽在打呃，卻是媽連回答也沒有一聲。

林小姐在牀上又翻一個身，翹起了頭，打算偷聽媽和誰談話，是那樣悄地放低了聲音。然而聽不清，只有媽的連聲打呃，間歇地

Ma's voice rose, as if she were angry, and a few words came through quite clearly:

" — These are Japanese goods, those are Japanese goods, hic! ..."

Miss Lin started. She prickled all over, like when she was having a hair-cut and the tiny shorn hairs stuck to her neck. She had come home annoyed just because they had laughed at her and scolded her at school over Japanese goods. She swept aside the little cat nestled against her, jumped up and stripped off her new azure rayon dress lined with camel's wool. She shook it out a couple of times, and sighed. Miss Lin had heard that this charming frock was made of Japanese material. She tossed it aside and pulled that cute cowhide case out from under the bed. Almost spitefully, she flipped the cover open, and turning the case upside down, dumped its contents on the bed. A rainbow of brightly coloured dresses and knick-knacks rolled and spread. The little cat leaped to the floor, whirled and jumped up on a chair, where he crouched and looked at his mistress in astonishment.

Miss Lin sorted through the pile of clothes, then stood, abstracted, beside the bed. The more she examined her belongings, the more she adored them — and the more they looked like Japanese goods! Couldn't she wear any of them? She hated to part with them — besides, her father wouldn't necessarily be willing to have new ones made for her! Miss Lin's eyes began to smart. She loved these Japanese things, while she hated the Japanese aggressors who invaded the Northeast provinces. If not for that, she could wear Japanese merchandise and no one would say a word.

"Hic — "

The sound came through the door, followed by the thin swaying body of Mrs. Lin. The sight of the heap of clothing on the bed, and her daughter, bemused, standing in only her brief woollen underwear,

飄到林小姐的耳朵。忽然媽的嗓音高了一些，似乎很生氣，就有幾個字聽得很分明：

——這也是東洋貨，那也是東洋貨，呃！……

林小姐猛一跳，就好像理髮時候頸脖子上粘了許多短頭髮似的渾身都煩躁起來了。正也是為了這東洋貨問題，她在學校裏給人家笑罵，她回家來沒好氣。她一手推開了又挨到她身邊來的小花，跳起來就剝下那件新製的翠綠色假毛葛駝絨旗袍來，拎在手裏抖了幾下，嘆一口氣。據說這怪好看的假毛葛和駝絨都是東洋來的。她撩開這件駝絨旗袍，從牀下拖出那口小巧的牛皮箱來，賭氣似的扭開了箱子蓋，把箱子底朝天向牀上一撒，花花綠綠的衣服和雜用品就滾滿了一牀。小花吃了一驚，噗的跳下牀去，轉一個身，卻又跳在一張椅子上蹲着望住牠的女主人。

林小姐的一雙手在那堆衣服裏抓撈了一會兒，就呆呆地站在牀前出神。這許多衣服和雜用品愈看愈可愛，卻又愈看愈像是東洋貨呢！全都不能穿了麼？可是她——捨不得，而且她的父親也未必肯另外再製新的！林小姐忍不住眼圈兒紅了。她愛這些東洋貨，她又恨那些東洋人；好好兒的發兵打東三省幹麼呢？不然，穿了東洋貨有誰來笑罵。

「呃——」

忽然房門邊來了這一聲。接着就是林大娘的搖搖擺擺的瘦身形。看見那亂丟了一牀的衣服，又看見女兒只穿着一件絨線短衣站

was more than a little shock. As her excitement increased, the tempo of Mrs. Lin's hiccups grew in proportion. For the moment, she was unable to speak. Miss Lin, grief written all over her face, flew to her mother. "Ma! They're all Japanese goods. What am I going to wear tomorrow?"

Hiccuping, Mrs. Lin shook her head. With one hand she supported herself on her daughter's shoulder, with the other she kneaded her own chest. After a while, she managed to force out a few sentences.

"Child — hic — why have you taken off — hic — all your clothes? The weather's cold — hic — This trouble of mine — hic — began the year you were born. Hic — lately it's getting worse! Hic — "

"Ma, tell me what am I going to wear tomorrow? I'll just hide in the house and not go out! They'll laugh at me, swear at me!"

Mrs. Lin didn't answer. Hiccuping steadily, she walked over to the bed, picked the new azure dress out of the pile, and draped it over her daughter. Then she patted the bed in invitation for Miss Lin to sit down. The little cat returned to beside the girl's legs. Cocking his head, with narrowed eyes he looked first at Mrs. Lin, then at her daughter. Lazily, he rolled over and rubbed his belly against the soles of the girl's shoes. Miss Lin kicked him away and reclined sideways on the bed, with her head hidden behind her mother's back.

Neither of them spoke for a while. Mrs. Lin was busy hiccuping; her daughter was busy calculating "how to go out tomorrow." The problem of Japanese goods not only affected everything Miss Lin wore — it influenced everything she used. Even the powder compact which her fellow students so admired and her automatic pencil were probably made in Japan. And she was crazy about those little gadgets!

"Child — hic — are you hungry?"

在牀前出神，林大娘這一驚非同小可。心裏愈是着急，她那個「呃」卻愈是打得多，暫時竟說不出半句話。

林小姐飛跑到母親身邊，哭喪着臉說：

「媽呀！全是東洋貨，明兒叫我穿什麼衣服？」

林大娘搖着頭只是打呃，一手扶住了女兒的肩膀，一手揉磨自己的胸脯，過了一會兒，她方才掙扎出幾句話來：

「阿囡，呃，你幹麼脫得——呃，光落落？留心凍——呃——我這毛病，呃，生你那年起了這個病痛，呃，近來愈發兇了！呃——」

「媽呀！你說明兒我穿什麼衣服？我只好躲在家裏不出去了，他們要笑我，罵我！」

但是林大娘不回答。她一路打呃，走到牀前揀出那件駝絨旗袍來，就替女兒披在身上，又拍拍牀，要她坐下。小花又挨到林小姐腳邊，昂起了頭，眯細着眼睛看看林大娘，又看看林小姐；然後牠懶懶地靠到林小姐的腳背上，就林小姐的鞋底來磨擦牠的肚皮。林小姐一腳踢開了小花，就勢身子一歪，躺在牀上，把臉藏在她母親的身後。

暫時兩個都沒有話。母親忙着打呃，女兒忙着盤算「明天怎樣出去」；這東洋貨問題不但影響到林小姐的所穿，還影響到她的所用；據說她那隻常為同學們艷羨的化妝皮夾以及自動鉛筆之類，也都是東洋貨，而她卻又愛這些小玩意兒的！

「阿囡，呃——肚子餓不餓？」林大娘坐定了半晌以後，漸漸少

After sitting quietly for some time, Mrs. Lin gradually controlled her hiccups, and began her usual doting routine.

"No. Ma, why do you always ask me if I'm hungry? The most important thing is that I have no clothes. How can I go to school tomorrow?" the girl demanded petulantly. She was still curled up on the bed, her face still buried behind her mother.

From the start, Mrs. Lin hadn't understood why her daughter kept complaining that she had no clothes to wear. This was the third time and she couldn't ignore the remark any longer, but those damned hiccups most irritatingly started up again. Just then, Mr. Lin came in. He was holding a sheet of paper in his hand; his face was ashen. He saw his wife struggling with continuous agitated hiccups, his daughter lying on the clothing-strewn bed, and he could guess pretty well what was wrong. His brows drew together in a frown.

"Do you have an Anti-Japanese-Invasion Society in your school, Xiu?" he asked. "This letter just came. It says that if you wear clothes made of Japanese material again tomorrow, they're going to burn them! Of all the wild lawless things to say!"

"Hic — hic!"

"What nonsense! Everyone has something made in Japan on him. But they have to pick on our family to make trouble! There isn't a shop carrying foreign goods that isn't full of Japanese stuff. But they have to make our shop the culprit. They insist on locking up our stocks! Huh! "

"Hic — hic — Goddess Guanyin protect and preserve us! Hic — "

"Papa, I've got an old style padded jacket. It's probably not made of Japanese material, but if I wear it they'll all laugh at me, it's so out of date," said Miss Lin, sitting up on the bed. She had been thinking of

打幾個呃了，就又開始她日常的疼愛女兒的老功課。

「不餓。噯，媽呀，怎麼老是問我餓不餓呢，頂要緊是沒有了衣服明天怎樣去上學！」

林小姐撒嬌說，依然那樣拳曲着身體躺着，依然把臉藏在母親背後。

自始就沒弄明白為甚麼女兒盡嚷着沒有衣服穿的林大娘現在第三次聽得了這話兒，不能不再注意了，可是她那該死的打呃很不作美地又連連來了。恰在此時林先生走了進來，手裏拿着一張字條兒，臉上烏霉霉地像是塗上一層灰。他看見林大娘不住地打呃，女兒躺在滿牀亂丟的衣服堆裏，他就料到了幾分，一雙眉頭就緊緊地皺起。他喚着女兒的名字說道：

「明秀，你的學校裏有什麼抗日會麼？剛送來了這封信。說是明天你再穿東洋貨的衣服去，他們就要燒呢——無法無天的話語，咳……」

「呃——呃！」

「真是豈有此理，哪一個人身上沒有東洋貨，卻偏偏找定了我們家來生事！哪一家洋廣貨鋪子裏不是堆足了東洋貨，偏是我的鋪子犯法，一定要封存！咄！」

林先生氣憤憤地又加了這幾句，就頹然坐在牀邊的一張椅子裏。

「呢，呃，救苦救難觀世音，呃——」

「爸爸，我還有一件老式的棉襖，光景不是東洋貨，可是穿出去人家又要笑我。」

過了一會兒，林小姐從牀上坐起來說，她本來打算進一步要求

going a step farther and asking Mr.Lin to have a dress made for her out of non-Japanese cloth, but his expression decided her against such a rash move. Still, picturing the jeers her old padded jacket would evoke, she couldn't restrain her tears.

"Hic — hic — child! — hic — don't cry — no one will laugh at you — hic — child.... "

"Xiu, you don't have to go to school tomorrow! We soon won't have anything to eat; how can we spend money on schools! " Mr. Lin was exasperated. He ripped up the letter and strode, sighing, from the room. Before long, he came hurrying back.

"Where's the key to the cabinet? Give it to me!" he demanded of his wife.

Mrs. Lin turned pale and stared at him. Her eternal hiccups were momentarily stilled.

"There's no help for it. We'll have to make an offering to those straying demons — " Mr. Lin paused to heave a sigh. "It'll cost me four hundred at most. If the Guomindang local branch thinks it's not enough, I'll quit doing business. Let them lock up the stocks! That shop opposite has more Japanese goods than I. They've made an investment of over ten thousand dollars. They paid out only five hundred, and they're going along without a bit of trouble. Five hundred dollars! Just mark it off as a couple of bad debts! The key! That gold necklace ought to bring about three hundred.... "

"Hic — hic — really, like a gang of robbers!" Mrs. Lin produced the key with a trembling hand. Tears streamed down her face. Miss Lin, however, did not cry. She was looking into space with misty eyes, recalling that Guomindang committeeman who had made a speech at her school, a hateful swarthy pockmarked fellow who stared at her like a hungry dog. She could picture him grasping the gold necklace

父親製一件不是東洋貨的新衣，但瞧着父親的臉色不對，便又不敢冒昧。同時，她的想像中就展開了那件舊棉襖惹人訕笑的情形，她忍不住哭起來了。

「呃，呃——啊喲！——呃，莫哭，——沒有人笑你——呃，阿囡……」

「阿秀，明天不用去讀書了！飯快要沒得吃了，還讀什麼書！」

林先生懊惱地説，把手裏那張字條兒扯得粉碎，一邊走出房去，一邊嘆氣跺腳。然而沒多幾時，林先生又匆匆地跑了回來，看着林大娘的面孔説道：

「櫥門上的鑰匙呢？給我！」

林大娘的臉色立刻變成灰白，瞪出了眼睛望着她的丈夫，永遠不放鬆她的打呃忽然靜定了半响。

「沒有辦法，只好去齋齋那些閒神野鬼了——」

林先生頓住了，嘆一口氣，然後又接下去説：

「至多我花四百塊。要是黨部裏還嫌少，我拚着不做生意，等他們來封！——我們對過的裕昌祥，進的東洋貨比我多，足足有一萬多塊錢的碼子呢，也只花了五百塊，就太平無事了。——五百塊！算是吃了幾筆倒賬罷！——鑰匙！咳！那一個金項圈，總可以兌成三百塊……」

「呃，呃，真——好比強盜！」

林大娘摸出那鑰匙來，手也顫抖了，眼淚撲簌簌地往下掉。林小姐卻反不哭了，瞪着一對淚眼，呆呆地出神，她恍惚看見那個曾經到她學校裏來演説而且餓狗似的盯住看她的什麼委員，一個怪叫

and jumping for joy, his big mouth open in a laugh. Then she visualized the ugly bandit quarrelling with her father, hitting him....

"Aiya!" Miss Lin gave a frightened scream and threw herself on her mother's bosom. Mrs. Lin was so started she had no time for hiccups.

"Child, hic — don't cry," Mrs. Lin made a desperate effort to speak. "After New Year your Papa will have money. We'll make a new dress for you, hic — Those black-hearted crooks! They all insist we have money. Hic — we lose more every year. Your Papa was in the fertilizer business, and he lost money, hic — Every penny invested in the shop belongs to other people. Child, hic, hic — this sickness of mine; it makes life hell — hic — In another two years when you're nineteen, we'll find you a good husband. Hic — then I can die in peace! Save us from our adversity, Goddess Guanyin! Hic — "

II

The following day, Mr. Lin's shop underwent a transformation. All the Japanese goods he hadn't dared to show for the past week, now were the most prominently displayed. In imitation of the big Shanghai stores, Mr. Lin inscribed many slips of coloured paper with the words "Big Sale 10% Discount!" and pasted them on his windows. Just seven days before New Year, this was the "rush season" of the shops selling imported goods in the towns and villages. Not only was there hope of earning back Mr. Lin's special expenditure of four hundred dollars; Miss Lin's new dress depended on the amount of business done in the next few days.

人討厭的黑麻子，捧住了她家的金項圈在半空裏跳，張開了大嘴巴
笑。隨後，她又恍惚看見這強盜似的黑麻子和她的父親吵嘴，父親
被他打了，……

「啊喲！」

林小姐猛然一聲驚叫，就撲在她媽的身上。林大娘慌得沒有工
夫盡打呃，掙扎着說：

「阿囡，呃，不要哭，——過了年，你爸爸有錢，就給你製新衣
服，——呃，那些狠心的強盜！都咬定我們有錢，呃，一年一年虧
空，你爸爸做做肥田粉生意又上當，呃——店裏全是別人的錢了。
阿囡，呃，呃，我這病，活着也受罪，——呃，再過兩年，你十九
歲，招得個好女婿。呃，我死也放心了！——救苦救難觀世音菩
薩！呃——」

第二天，林先生的鋪子裏新換過一番佈置。將近一星期不曾露
臉的東洋貨又都擺在最惹眼的地位了。林先生又摹仿上海大商店的
辦法，寫了許多「大廉價照碼九折」的紅綠紙條，貼在玻璃窗上。這
天是陰曆臘月二十三，正是鄉鎮上洋廣貨店的「旺月」。不但林先生
的額外支出「四百元」指望在這時候撈回來，就是林小姐的新衣服也
靠托在這幾天的生意好。

A little past ten in the morning, group of peasants who had come into town to sell their produce in the market began drifting along the street. Carrying baskets on their arms, leading small children, they chatted loud and vigorously as they strolled. They stopped to look at the red and green blurbs pasted on Mr. Lin's windows and called attention to them, women shouting to their husbands, children yelling to their parents, clucking their tongues in admiration over the goods on display in the shop windows. It would soon be New Year. Children were wishing for a pair of new socks. Women remembered that the family wash-basin had been broken for some time. The single washcloth used by the entire family had been bought half a year ago, and now was an old rag. They had run out of soap more than a month before. They ought to take advantage of this "Sale" and buy a few things.

Mr. Lin sat in the cashier's cage, marshalling all his energies, a broad smile plastered on his face. He watched the peasants, while keeping an eye on his two salesmen and two apprentices. With all his heart he hoped to see his merchandise start moving out and the silver dollars begin rolling in.

But these peasants, after looking a while, after pointing and gesticulating appreciatively a while, ambled over to the store across the street to stand and look some more. Craning his neck, Mr. Lin glared at the backs of the group of peasants, and sparks shot from his eyes. He wanted to go over and drag them back!

"Hic — hic — "

Behind the cashier's cage were swinging doors which separated the shop itself from the "inner sanctum." "Beside these doors sat Mrs. Lin releasing hiccups that she had long been suppressing with difficulty. Miss Lin was seated beside her. Entranced, the girl watched

十點多鐘，趕市的鄉下人一群一群的在街上走過了，他們臂上挽着籃，或是牽着小孩子，粗聲大氣地一邊在走，一邊在談話。他們望到了林先生的花花綠綠的鋪面，都站住了，仰起臉，老婆喚丈夫，孩子叫爹娘，嘖嘖地誇羨那些貨物。新年快到了，孩子們希望穿一雙新襪子，女人們想到家裏的面盆早就用破，全家合用的一條面巾還是半年前的老傢伙，肥皂又斷絕了一個多月，趁這裏「賣賤貨」，正該買一點。林先生坐在賬台上，抖擻着精神，堆起滿臉的笑容，眼睛望着那些鄉下人，又帶睄着自己鋪子裏的兩個夥計，兩個學徒，滿心希望貨物出去，洋錢進來。但是這些鄉下人看了一會，指指點點誇羨了一會，竟自懶洋洋地走到斜對門的裕昌祥鋪面前站住了再看。林先生伸長了脖子，望到那班鄉下人的背影，眼睛裏冒出火來。他恨不得拉他們回來！

「呃——呃——」

坐在賬台後面那道分隔鋪面與「內宅」的蝴蝶門旁邊的林大娘把勉強忍住了半晌的「呃」放出來。林小姐倚在她媽的身邊，呆呆地望

the street silently, her heart pounding. At least half of her new dress had just walked away.

Mr. Lin strode quickly to the front of the counter. He glared jealously at the shop opposite. Its five salesmen were waiting expectantly behind the counter. But not one peasant entered the store. They looked for a while, then continued on their way. Mr. Lin relaxed; he couldn't help grinning at the salesmen across the street. Another group of seven or eight peasants stopped before Mr. Lin's shop. A youngster among them actually came a step forward. With his head cocked to one side, he examined the imported umbrellas. Mr. Lin whirled around, his face breaking into a happy smile. He went to work personally on this prospective customer.

"Would you like a foreign umbrella, Brother? They're cheap. You only pay ninety cents on the dollar. Come and take a look."

A salesman had already taken down two or three imported umbrellas. He promptly opened one and shoved it earnestly into the young peasant's hand. Summoning all his zeal, the salesman launched into a high powered patter:

"Just look at this, young master! Foreign satin cloth, solid ribs. It's durable and handsome for rainy days or clear. Ninety cents each. They don't come any cheaper.... Across the street, they're a dollar apiece, but they're not as good as these. You can compare them and see why."

The young peasant held the umbrella and stood undecided, with his mouth open. He turned towards a man in his fifties and weighed the umbrella in his hand as if to ask "Shall I buy it?" The older man became very upset and began to shout at him.

"You're crazy! Buying an umbrella! We only got three dollars for the whole boatload of firewood, and your mother's waiting at home

着街上不作聲，心頭卻是卜卜地跳；她的新衣服至少已經走脫了半件。

林先生趕到櫃台前睜大了妒忌的眼睛看着斜對門的同業裕昌祥。那邊的四五個店員一字兒擺在櫃台前，等候做買賣。但是那班鄉下人沒有一個走近到櫃台邊，他們看了一會兒，又照樣的走過去了。林先生覺得心頭一鬆，忍不住望着裕昌祥的夥計笑了一笑。這時又有七八人一隊的鄉下人走到林先生的鋪面前，其中有一位年青的居然上前一步，歪着頭看那些掛着的洋傘。林先生猛轉過臉來，一對嘴唇皮立刻嘻開了；他親自兜攬這位意想中的顧客了：

「喂，阿弟，買洋傘麼？便宜貨，一隻洋賣九角！看看貨色去。」

一個夥計已經取下了兩三把洋傘，立刻撐開了一把，熱剌剌地塞到那年青鄉下人的手裏，振起精神，使出誇賣的本領來：

「小當家，你看！洋緞面子，實心骨子，晴天，落雨，耐用好看！九角洋錢一頂，再便宜沒有了！……那邊是一隻洋一頂，貨色還沒有這等好呢，你比一比就明白。」

那年青的鄉下人拿着傘，沒有主意似的張大了嘴巴。他回過頭去望着一位五十多歲的老頭子，又把手裏的傘攔了一攔，似乎說：「買一把罷？」老頭子卻老大着急地吆喝道：

「阿大！你昏了，想買傘！一船硬柴，一古腦兒只賣了三塊多

for us to bring back some rice. How can you spend money on an umbrella!"

"It's cheap, but we can't afford it!" sighed the peasants standing around watching. They walked slowly away. The young peasant, his face brick red, shook his head. He put down the umbrella and started to leave. Mr. Lin was frantic. He quickly gave ground.

"How much do you say, Brother? Take another look. It's fine merchandise!"

"It is cheap. But we don't have enough money," the older peasant replied, pulling his son. They practically ran away.

Bitterly, Mr. Lin returned to the cashier's cage, feeling weak all over. He knew it wasn't that he was an inept businessman. The peasants simply were too poor. They couldn't even spend ninety cents on an umbrella. He stole a glance at the shop across the way. There too people were looking, but no one was going in. In front of the neighbouring grocery store and the cookie shop, no one was even looking. Group after group of the country folk walked by carrying baskets. But the baskets all were empty. Occasionally, someone appeared with a homespun flowered blue cloth sack, filled with rice, from the look of it. The late rice which the peasants had harvested more than a month before had long since been squeezed out as rent for the landlords and interest for the usurers. Now in order to have rice to eat, the peasants were forced to buy a measure or two at a time, at steep prices.

All this Mr. Lin knew. He felt that at least part of his business was being indirectly eaten away by the usurers and landlords.

The hour gradually neared noon. There were very few peasants on the street now. Mr. Lin's shop had done a little over one dollar's worth of business, just enough to cover the cost of the "Big Sale 10%

錢，你娘等着量米回去吃，哪有錢來買傘！」

「貨色是便宜，沒有錢買！」

站在那裏觀望的鄉下人都嘆着氣說，懶洋洋地都走了。那年青的鄉下人滿臉漲紅，搖一下頭，放了傘也就要想走，這可把林先生急壞了，趕快讓步問道：

「喂，喂，阿弟，你說多少錢呢？——再看看去，貨色是靠得住的！」

「貨色是便宜，錢不夠。」

老頭子一面回答，一面拉住了他的兒子，逃也似的走了。林先生苦着臉，踱回到賬台裏，渾身不得勁兒。他知道不是自己不會做生意，委實是鄉下人太窮了，買不起九毛錢的一頂傘。他偷眼再望斜對門的裕昌祥，也還是只有人站在那裏看，沒有人上櫃台買。裕昌祥左右鄰的生泰雜貨店萬姓糕餅店那就簡直連看的人都沒有半個。一群一群走過的鄉下人都挽着籃子，但籃子裏空無一物；間或有花藍布的一包兒，看樣子就知道是米：甚至一個多月前鄉下人收穫的晚稻也早已被地主們和高利貸的債主們如數逼光，現在鄉下人不得不一升兩升的量着貴米吃。這一切，林先生都明白，他就覺得自己的一份生意至少是間接的被地主和高利貸者剝奪去了。

時間漸漸移近正午，街上走的鄉下人已經很少了，林先生的鋪子就只做成了一塊多錢的生意，僅僅足夠開銷了「大廉價照碼九折」

Discount" strips of red and green paper. Despondently, Mr. Lin entered the "inner sanctum." He barely had the courage to face his wife and daughter. Miss Lin's eyes were filled with tears. She sat in the corner with her head down. Mrs. Lin was in the middle of a string of hiccups. Struggling for control, she addressed her husband.

"We laid out four hundred dollars — and spent all night getting things ready in the shop — hic! We got permission to sell the Japanese goods, but business is dead — hic — my blessed ancestors! ... The maid wants her wages — "

"It's only half a day. Don't worry." Mr. Lin forced a comforting note into his voice, but he felt worse than if a knife were cutting through his heart. Gloomily, he paced back and forth. He thought of all the business promotion tricks he knew, but none of them seemed any good. Business was bad. It had been bad in all lines for some time; his shop wasn't the only one having difficulty. People were poor, and there wasn't anything that could be done about it. Still, he hoped business would be better in the afternoon. The local townspeople usually did their buying then. Surely they would buy things for New Year! If only they wanted to buy, Mr. Lin's shop was certain of trade. After all, his merchandise was cheaper than other shops!

It was this hope that enabled Mr. Lin to bolster his sagging spirits as he sat in the cashier's cage awaiting the customers he pictured coming in the afternoon.

And the afternoon proved to be different indeed from the morning. There weren't many people on the street, but Mr. Lin knew nearly every one of them. He knew their names, or the names of their fathers or grandfathers. These were local townspeople, and as they chatted and walked slowly past his shop, Mr. Lin's eyes, glowing with cordiality, welcomed them, and sent them on their way. At times, with a broad smile he greeted an old customer.

的紅綠紙條的廣告費。林先生垂頭喪氣走進「內宅」去，幾乎沒有勇氣和女兒老婆相見。林小姐含着一泡眼淚，低着頭坐在屋角；林大娘在一連串的打呃中，掙扎着對丈夫説：

「花了四百塊錢，——又忙了一個晚上擺設起來，呃，東洋貨是准賣了，卻又生意清淡，呃——阿囡的爺呀！……吳媽又要拿工錢——」

「還只半天呢！不要着急。」

林先生勉強安慰着，心裏的難受，比刀割還厲害。他悶悶地踱了幾步。所有推廣營業的方法都想遍了，覺得都不是路。生意清淡，早已各業如此，並不是他一家呀；人們都窮了，可沒有法子。但是他總還希望下午的營業能夠比較好些。本鎮的人家買東西大概在下午。難道他們過新年不買些東西？只要他們存心買，林先生的營業是有把握的。畢竟他的貨物比別家便宜。

是這盼望使得林先生依然能夠抖擻着精神坐在賬台上守候他意想中的下午的顧客。

這下午照例和上午顯然不同：街上並沒很多的人，但幾乎每個人都相識，都能夠叫出他們的姓名，或是他們的父親和祖父的姓名。林先生靠在櫃台上，用了異常溫和的眼光迎送這些慢慢地走着談着經過他那鋪面的本鎮人。他時常笑嘻嘻地迎着常有交易的人喊道：

"Ah, Brother, going out to the tea-house? Our little shop has slashed its prices. Favour us with a small purchase!"

Sometimes, the man would actually stop and come into the shop. Then Mr. Lin and his assistants would plunge into a frenzy of activity. With acute sensitiveness, they would watch the eyes of the unpredictable customer. The moment his eyes rested on a piece of merchandise, the salesmen would swiftly produce one just like it and invite the customer to examine it. Miss Lin watched from beside the swinging doors, and her father frequently called her out to respectfully greet the unpredictable customer as "Uncle." An apprentice would serve him a glass of tea and offer him a good cigarette.

On the question of price, Mr. Lin was exceptionally flexible. When a customer was firm about knocking off a few odd cents from the round figure of his purchase price, Mr. Lin would take the abacus from the hands of his salesman and calculate personally. Then, with the air of a man who has been driven to the wall, he would deduct the few odd cents from the total bill.

"We'll take a loss on this sale," he would say with a wry smile. "But you're an old customer. We have to please you. Come and buy some more things soon!"

The entire afternoon was spent in this manner. Including cash and credit, big purchases and small, the shop made a total of over ten sales. Mr. Lin was drenched with perspiration, and although he was worn out, he was very happy. He had been sneaking looks at the shop across the street. They didn't seem to be nearly so busy. There was a pleased expression on the face of Miss Lin, who had been constantly watching from beside the swinging doors. Mrs. Lin even jerked out a few less hiccups.

Shortly before dark, Mr. Lin finished adding up his accounts for

「呵，××哥，到清風閣去吃茶麼？小店大放盤，交易點兒去！」

有時被喚着的那位居然站住了，走上櫃台來，於是林先生和他的店員就要大忙而特忙，異常敏感地伺察着這位未可知的顧客的眼光，瞧見他的眼光瞥到什麼貨物上，就趕快拿出那種貨物請他考較。林小姐站在那對蝴蝶門邊看望，也常常被林先生喚出來對那位未可知的顧客叫一聲「伯伯」。小學徒送上一杯便茶來，外加一枝小聯珠。

在價目上，林先生也格外讓步；遇到那位顧客一定要除去一毛錢左右尾數的時候，他就從店員手裏拿過那算盤來算了一會兒，然後不得已似的把那尾數從算盤上撥去，一面笑嘻嘻地說：

「真不夠本呢！可是老主顧，只好遵命了。請你多作成幾筆生意罷！」整個下午就是這麼張羅着過去了。連現帶賒，大大小小，居然也有十來注交易。林先生早已汗透棉袍。雖然是累得那麼着，林先生心裏卻很愉快。他冷眼偷看斜對門的裕昌祥，似乎趕不上自己鋪子的「熱鬧」。常在那對蝴蝶門旁邊看望的林小姐臉上也有些笑意，林大娘也少打幾個呃了。

快到上燈時候，林先生核算這一天的「流水賬」；上午等於零，

the day. The morning amounted to zero; in the afternoon they had sold sixteen dollars and eighty-five cents worth of merchandise, eight dollars of it being on credit. Mr. Lin smiled sligtly, then he frowned. He had been selling all his goods at their original cost. He hadn't even covered his expenses for the day, to say nothing of making any profit. His mind was blank for a moment. Then he took out his account books and calculated in them for a long time. On the "credit" side there was a total of over thirteen hundred dollars of uncollected debts — more than six hundred in town and over seven hundred in the countryside. But the "debit" ledger showed a figure of eight hundred dollars owed to the big Shanghai wholesale house alone. He owed a total of not less than two thousand dollars!

Mr. Lin sighed softly. If business continued to be so bad, it was going to be a little difficult for him to get through New Year. He looked at the red and green paper slips on the window announcing "Big Sale 10% Discount." If we really cut prices like we did today, business ought to pick up, he thought to himself. We're not making any profit, but if we don't do any business I still have to pay expenses anyway. The main thing is to get the customers to come in, then I can gradually raise my prices.... If we can do some wholesale business in the countryside, that will be even better! ...

Suddenly, someone broke in on Mr. Lin's sweet dream. A shaky old lady entered the shop carrying a little bundle wrapped in blue cloth. Mr. Lin yanked up his head to find her confronting him. He wanted to escape, but there was no time. He could only go forward and greet her.

"Ah, Mrs. Zhu, out buying things for the New Year? Please come into the back room and sit down. — Xiu, give Mrs. Chu your arm."

But Miss Lin didn't hear. She had left the swinging doors some time ago. Mrs. Zhu waved her hand in refusal and sat down on a chair

下午賣了十六元八角五分，八塊錢是賒賬。林先生微微一笑，但立即皺緊了眉頭了；他今天的「大放盤」確是照本出賣，開銷都沒着落，官利更說不上。他呆了一會兒，又開了賬箱，取出幾本賬簿來翻着打了半天算盤；賬上「人欠」的數目共有一千三百餘元，本鎮六百多，四鄉七百多；可是「欠人」的客賬，單是上海的東昇字號就有八百，合計不下二千哪！林先生低聲嘆一口氣，覺得明天以後如果生意依然沒見好，那他這年關就有點難過了。他望着玻璃窗上「大放盤照碼九折」的紅綠紙條，心裏這麼想：「照今天那樣當真放盤，生意總該會見好；虧本麼？沒有生意也是照樣的要開銷。只好先拉些主顧來再慢慢兒想法提高貨碼……要是四鄉還有批發生意來，那就更好！──」

突然有一個人來打斷林先生的甜蜜夢想了。這是五十多歲的一位老婆子，巍顫顫地走進店來，手裏拿着一個小小的藍布包。林先生猛抬起頭來，正和那老婆子打一個照面，想躲避也躲避不及，只好走上前去招呼她道：

「朱三太，出來買過年東西麼？請到裏面去坐坐。──阿秀，來扶朱三太。」

林小姐早已不在那對蝴蝶門邊了，沒有聽到。那朱三太連連搖手，就在鋪面裏的一張椅子上坐了，鄭重地打開她的藍布手巾包，

in the store. Solemnly, she unwrapped the blue cloth and brought out a small account book. With two trembling hands she presented the book under Mr. Lin's nose. Twisting her withered lips, she was about to speak, but Mr. Lin had already taken the book and was hastening to say:

"I understand, I'll send it to your house tomorrow."

"Mm, mm, the tenth month, the eleventh month, the twelfth month; altogether three months. Three threes are nine; that's nine dollars, isn't it? — you'll send the money tomorrow? Mm, mm, you don't have to send it. I'll take it back with me! Eh!"

The words seemed to come with difficulty from Mrs. Zhu's withered mouth. She had three hundred dollars loaned to Mr. Lin's shop, and was entitled to three dollars interest every month. Mr. Lin had delayed payment for three months, promising to pay in full at the end of the year. Now, she needed some money to buy gifts for tomorrow's Kitchen God Festival, and so she had come seeking Mr. Lin. From the forcefulness with which she moved her puckered mouth, Mr. Lin could tell that she was determined not to leave without the money.

Mr. Lin scratched his head in silence. He hadn't been deliberately refusing to pay the interest. It was just that for the past three months business had been poor. Their daily sales had been barely enough to cover their food and taxes. He had delayed paying her unconsciously. But if he didn't pay her today, the old lady might raise a row in the shop. That would be too shameful and would seriously influence the shop's future.

"All right, all right. Take it back with you!" Mr. Lin finally said in exasperation. His voice shook a little. He rushed to the cashier's cage and gathered together all the cash that had been taken in that morning and afternoon. To that he added twenty cents from his own pocket,

——包裹僅有一扣摺子，她抖抖簌簌地雙手捧了，直送到林先生的鼻子前，她的癟嘴唇扭了幾扭，正想說話，林先生早已一手接過那摺子，同時搶先說道；

「我曉得了。明天送到你府上罷。」

「哦，哦；十月，十一月，十二月，一總是三個月，三三得九，是九塊罷？——明天你送來？哦，哦，不要送，讓我帶了去。嗯！」

朱三太扭着她的癟嘴唇，很艱難似的說。她有三百元的「老本」存在林先生的鋪裏，按月來取三塊錢的利息，可是最近林先生卻拖欠了三個月，原說是到了年底總付，明天是送灶日，老婆子要買送灶的東西，所以親自上林先生的鋪子來了。看她那股扭起了一對癟嘴唇的勁兒，光景是錢不到手就一定不肯走。

林先生抓着頭皮不作聲。這九塊錢的利息，他何嘗存心白賴，只是三個月來生意清淡，每天賣得的錢僅夠開伙食，付捐稅，不知不覺就拖欠下來了。然而今天要是不付，這老婆子也許會就在鋪面上嚷鬧，那就太丟臉，對於營業的前途很有影響。

「好，好，帶了去罷，帶了去罷！」

林先生終於鬥氣似的說，聲音有點兒哽咽。他跑到賬台裏，把上下午賣得的現錢歸併起來，又從腰包裏掏出一個雙毫，這才湊成

and presented the whole collection of dollars, pennies and dimes to the old lady. She carefully counted the lot over and over again, then with trembling hands wrapped the money in the blue cloth. Mr. Lin couldn't repress a sigh. He had a wild desire to snatch back a part of the cash.

"That blue handkerchief is too worn, Mrs. Zhu," he said with a forced laugh. "Why not buy a good white linen one? We've also got top quality wash-cloths and soap. Take some to use over the New Year. Prices are reasonable!"

"No, I don't want any. An old lady like me doesn't need that kind of thing." She waved her hand in refusal. She put her account book in her pocket and departed, firmly grasping the blue cloth bundle.

Looking sour, Mr. Lin walked into the "inner sanctum." Mrs. Zhu's visit reminded him that he had two other creditors. Old Chen and Widow Zhang had put up two hundred and one hundred and fifty dollars respectively. He would have to pay them a total of ten dollars interest. He couldn't very well delay their money; in fact, he would have to pay them ahead of time. He counted on his fingers — twenty-fourth, twenty-fifth, twenty-sixth. By the twenty-sixth, he ought to be able to collect all the outstanding debts in the countryside. His clerk Shousheng had gone off on a collection trip the day before yesterday. He should be back by the twenty-sixth at the latest. The unpaid bills in town couldn't be collected till the twenty-eighth or twenty-ninth. But the collector from the Shanghai wholesale house to which Mr. Lin owed money would probably come tomorrow or the day after. Lin's only alternative was to borrow more from the local bank. And how would business be tomorrow? ...

His head down, Mr. Lin paced back and forth, thinking. The voice of his daughter spoke into his ear:

了八塊大洋，十角小洋，四十個銅子，交付了朱三太。當他看見那老婆子把這些銀洋銅子鄭重地數了又數，而且抖抖簌簌地放在那藍布手巾上包了起來的時候，他忍不住嘆一口氣，異想天開地打算拉回幾文來；他勉強笑着說：

「三阿太，你這藍布手巾太舊了，買一塊老牌麻紗白手帕去罷？我們有上好的洗臉手巾，肥皂，買一點兒去新年裏用罷。價錢公道！」

「不要，不要；老太婆了，用不到。」

朱三太連連搖手說，把摺子藏在衣袋裏，捧着她的藍布手巾包竟自去了。

林先生哭喪着臉，走回「內宅」去。因這朱三太的上門討利息，他記起還有兩注存款，橋頭陳老七的二百元和張寡婦的一百五十元，總共十來塊錢的利息，都是「不便」拖欠的，總得先期送去。他搯着指頭算日子：二十四，二十五，二十六——到二十六，放在四鄉的賬頭該可以收齊了，店裏的壽生是前天出去收賬的，極遲是二十六應該回來了；本鎮的賬頭總得到二十八九方才有個數目。然而上海號家的收賬客人說不定明後天就會到，只有再向恆源錢莊去借了。但是明天的門市怎樣？……

他這麼低着頭一邊走，一邊想，猛聽得女兒的聲音在他耳邊說：

"Papa, what do you think of this piece of silk? Four dollars and twenty cents for seven feet. That's not expensive, is it?"

Mr. Lin's heart gave a leap. He stood stock-still and glared, speechless. Miss Lin held the piece of silk in her hand and giggled. Four dollars and twenty cents! It wasn't a big sum, but the shop only did sixteen dollars worth of business all day, and really at cost price! Mr. Lin stood frozen, then asked weakly:

"Where did you get the money?"

"I put it on the books."

Another debit. Mr. Lin scowled. But he had spoiled his daughter himself, and Mrs. Lin would take the girl's side no matter what the case might be. He smiled a helpless bitter smile. Then he sighed.

"You're always in such a rush," he said, slightly reproving. "Why couldn't you wait till after New Year!"

III

Another two days went by. Business was indeed very brisk in Mr. Lin's shop, with its "Big Sale." They did over thirty dollars in sales every day. The hiccups of Mrs. Lin diminished considerably; she hiccuped on the average of only once every five minutes. Miss Lin skipped up and back between the shop and the "inner sanctum," her face flushed and smiling. At times she even helped with the selling. Only after her mother called her repeatedly, did she return to the back room. Mopping her brow, she protested excitedly.

「爸爸，你看這塊大綢好麼？七尺，四塊二角，不貴罷？」

林先生心裏驀地一跳，站住了睜大着眼睛，說不出話。林小姐手裏托着那塊綢，卻在那裏憨笑。四塊二角！數目可真不算大，然而今天店裏總共只賣得十六塊多，並且是老實照本賤賣的呀！林先生怔了一會兒，這才沒精打彩地問道：

「你哪來的錢呢？」

「掛在賬上。」

林先生聽得又是欠賬，忍不住皺一下眉頭。但女兒是自己寵慣了的，林大娘又抵死偏護着，林先生沒奈何只有苦笑。過一會兒，他嘆一口氣，輕輕埋怨道：

「那麼性急！過了年再買豈不是好！」

又過了兩天，「大放盤」的林先生的鋪子，生意果然很好，每天可以做三十多元的生意了。林大娘的打呃，大大減少，平均是五分鐘來一次；林小姐在鋪面和「內宅」之間跳進跳出，臉上紅噴噴地時常在笑，有時竟在鋪面幫忙招呼生意，直到林大娘再三喚她，方才跑進去，一邊擦着額上的汗珠，一邊興沖沖地急口說：

"Ma, why have you called me back again? It's not hard work! Ma, Papa's so tired he's soaking wet; his voice is gone! — A customer just made a five-dollar purchase! Ma, you don't have to be afraid it's too tiring for me! Don't worry! Papa told me to rest a while, then come out again!"

Mrs. Lin only nodded her head and hiccuped, followed by a murmur that "Buddha is merciful and kind." A porcelain image of the Goddess Guanyin was enshrined in the "inner sanctum," with a stick of incense burning before it. Mrs. Lin swayed over to the shrine and kowtowed. She thanked the Goddess for Her Protection and prayed for Her Blessing on a number of matters — that Mr. Lin's business should always be good, that Miss Lin should grow nicely, that next year the girl should get a good husband.

But out in the shop, although Mr. Lin was devoting his whole being to business, though a smile never left his face, he felt as if his heart were bound with strings. Watching the satisfied customer going out with a package under his arm, Mr. Lin suffered a pang with every dollar he took in, as the abacus in his mind clicked a five per cent loss off the cost price he had raised through sweat and blood. Several times he tried to estimate the loss as being three per cent, but no matter how he figured it, he still was losing five cents on the dollar. Although business was good, the more he sold the worse he felt. As he waited on the customers, the conflict raging within his breast at times made him nearly faint. When he stole glances at the shop across the street, he had the impression that the owner and salesmen were sneering at him from behind their counters. Look at that fool Lin! they seemed to be saying. He really *is* selling below cost! Wait and see! The more business he does, the more he loses! The sooner he'll have to close down!

Mr. Lin gnawed his lips. He vowed he would raise his prices the

「媽呀，又叫我進來幹麼！我不覺得辛苦呀！媽！爸爸累得滿身是汗，嗓子也喊啞了！——剛才一個客人買了五塊錢東西呢！媽！不要怕我辛苦，不要怕！爸爸叫我歇一會兒就出去呢！」

林大娘只是點頭，打一個呃，就唸一聲「大慈大悲菩薩」。客廳裏本就供奉着一尊瓷觀音，點着一炷香，林大娘就搖搖擺擺走過去磕頭，謝菩薩的保祐，還要禱告菩薩一發慈悲，保佑林先生的生意永遠那麼好，保祐林小姐易長易大，明年就得個好女婿。

但是在鋪面張羅的林先生雖然打起精神做生意，臉上笑容不斷，心裏卻像有幾根線牽着。每逢賣得了一塊錢，看見顧客欣然挾着紙包而去，林先生就忍不住心裏一頓，在他心裏的算盤上就加添了五分洋錢的血本的虧折。他幾次想把這個「大放盤」時每塊錢的實足虧折算成三分，可是無論如何，算來算去總得五分。生意雖然好，他卻愈賣愈心疼了。在櫃台上招呼主顧的時候，他這種矛盾的心理有時竟至幾乎使他發暈。偶爾他偷眼望望斜對門的裕昌祥，就覺得那邊閒立在櫃台邊的店員和掌櫃，嘴角上都帶着譏諷的訕笑，似乎都在說：「看這姓林的傻子呀，當真虧本放盤哪！看着罷，他的生意愈好，就愈虧本，倒閉得愈快！」那時候，林先生便咬一下嘴

next day. He would charge first-grade prices for second-rate merchandise.

The head of the Merchants Guild came by. It was he who had interceded with the Guomindang chieftains for Mr. Lin on the question of selling Japanese goods. Now he smiled and congratulated Mr. Lin, and clapped him on the shoulder.

"How goes it? That four hundred dollars was well spent!" he said softly. "But you'd better give a small token to Guomindang Party Commissioner Bu too. Otherwise, he may become annoyed and try to squeeze you. When business is good, plenty of people are jealous. Even if Commissioner Bu doesn't have any 'ideas,' they'll try to stir him up!"

Mr. Lin thanked the head of the Merchants Guild for his concern. Inwardly, he was very alarmed. He almost lost his zest for doing business.

What made him most uneasy was that his assistant Shousheng still hadn't returned from the bill collecting trip. He needed the money to pay off his account with the big Shanghai wholesale house. The collector had arrived from Shanghai two days before, and was pressing Mr. Lin hard. If Shousheng didn't come soon, Mr. Lin would have to borrow from the local bank. This would mean an additional burden of fifty or sixty dollars in interest payments. To Mr. Lin, losing money every day, this prospect was more painful than being flayed alive.

At about four p.m., Mr. Lin suddenly heard a noisy uproar on the street. People looked very frightened, as though some serious calamity had happened. Mr. Lin, who could think only of whether Shousheng would safely return, was sure that the river boat on which Shousheng would come back had been set upon by pirates. His heart pounding, he hailed a passer-by and asked worriedly:

"What's wrong? Did pirates get the boat from Lishi?"

唇，決定明天無論如何要把貨碼提高，要把次等貨標上頭等貨的價格。

給林先生斡旋那「封存東洋貨」問題的商會長當走過林家鋪子的時候，也微微笑着，站住了對林先生賀喜，並且拍着林先生的肩膀，輕聲說：

「如何？四百塊錢是花得不冤枉罷！——可是，卜局長那邊，你也得稍稍點綴，防他看得眼紅，也要來敲詐。生意好，妒忌的人就多；就是卜局長不生心，他們也要去挑撥呀！」林先生謝商會長的關切，心裏老大吃驚，幾乎連做生意都沒有精神。

然而最使他心神不寧的，是店裏的壽生出去收賬到現在還沒有回來，林先生是等着壽生收的錢來開銷「客賬」。上海東昇字號的收賬客人前天早已到鎮，直催逼得林先生再沒有話語支吾了。如果壽生再不來，林先生只有向恆源錢莊借款的一法，這一來，林先生又將多負擔五六十元的利息，這在見天虧本的林先生委實比割肉還心疼。

到四點鐘光景，林先生忽然聽得街上走過的人們亂哄哄地在議論着什麼，人們的臉色都很惶急，似乎發生了什麼大事情了。一心惦念着出去收賬的壽生是否平安的林先生就以為一定是快班船遭了強盜搶，他的心卜卜地亂跳。他喚住了一個路人焦急地問道：

「什麼事？是不是栗市快班遭了強盜搶？」

"Oh! So it's pirates again? Travelling is really too dangerous! Robbing is nothing. Men are even kindnapped right off the boat!" babbled the passer-by, a well-known loafer named Lu. He eyed the brightly coloured goods in the shop.

Mr. Lin could make no sense out of this at all. His worry increased and he dropped Lu to accost Wang, the next person who came along.

"Is it true that the boat from Lishi was robbed?"

"It must be A Shu's gang that did it. A Shu has been shot, but his gang is still a tough bunch!" Wang replied without slackening his pace.

Cold sweat bedewed Mr. Lin's forehead. He was frantic. He was sure that Shousheng was coming back today, and from Lishi. That was the last place on the account book list. Now it was already four o'clock, but there was no sign of Shousheng. After what Wang had said, how could Mr. Lin have any doubts? He forgot that he himself had invented the story of the boat being robbed. His whole face beaded with perspiration, he rushed into the "inner sanctum." Going through the swinging doors, he tripped over the threshold and nearly fell.

"Papa, they're fighting in Shanghai! The Japanese bombed the Zhabei section!" cried Miss Lin, running up to him.

Mr. Lin stopped short. What was all this about fighting in Shanghai? His first reaction was that it had nothing to do with him. But since it involved the "Japanese," he thought he had better inquire a little further. Looking at his daughter's agitated face, he asked:

"The Japanese bombed it? Who told you that?"

"Everyone on the street is talking about it. The Japanese soldiers fired heavy artillery and they bombed. Zhabei is burned to the ground!"

「哦！又是強盜搶麼？路上真不太平！搶，還是小事，還要綁人去哪！」

那人，有名的閒漢陸和尚，含糊地回答，同時睬着半隻眼睛看林先生鋪子裏花花綠綠的貨物。林先生不得要領，心裏更急，丟開陸和尚，就去問第二個走近來的人，橋頭的王三毛。

「聽說栗市班遭搶，當真麼？」

「那一定是太保阿書手下人幹的，太保阿書是槍斃了，他的手下人多麼厲害！」

王三毛一邊回答，一邊只顧走。可是林先生卻急壞了，冷汗從額角上鑽出來。他早就估量到壽生一定是今天回來，而且是從栗市——收賬程序中預定的最後一處，坐快班船回來；此刻已是四點鐘，不見他來，王三毛又是那樣說，那還有什麼疑義麼？林先生竟忘記了這所謂「栗市班遭強盜搶」乃是自己的發明了！他滿臉急汗，直往「內宅」跑；在那對蝴蝶門邊忘記跨門檻，幾乎絆了一交。

「爸爸！上海打仗了！東洋兵放炸彈燒閘北——」

林小姐大叫着跑到林先生跟前。

林先生怔了一下。什麼上海打仗，原就和他不相干，但中間既然牽連着「東洋兵」，又好像不能不追問一聲了。他看着女兒的很興奮的臉孔問道：

「東洋兵放炸彈麼？你從哪裏聽來的？」

「街上走過的人全是那麼說。東洋兵放大炮，擲炸彈。閘北燒光了！」

"Oh, well, did anyone say that the boat from Lishi was robbed?"

Miss Lin shook her head, then fluttered from the room like a moth. Mr. Lin hesitated beside the swinging doors, scratching his head. Mrs. Lin was hiccuping and mumbling prayers.

"Buddha protect us! Don't let any bombs fall on our heads!"

Mr. Lin turned and went out to the shop. He saw his daughter engaged in excited conversation with the two salesmen. The owner of the shop across the street had come out from behind his counter and was talking, gesticulating wildly. There was fighting in Shanghai; Japanese planes had bombed Zhabei and burned it; the merchants in Shanghai had closed down — it all was true. What about the pirates robbing the boat? No one had heard anything about that! And the boat from Lishi? It had come in safely. The shopowner across the street had just seen stevedores from the boat going by with two big crates. Mr. Lin was relieved. Shousheng hadn't come back today, but he hadn't been robbed by pirates either!

Now the whole town was talking about the catastrophe in Shanghai. Young clerks were cursing the Japanese aggressors. People were even shouting, "Anyone who buys Japanese goods is a son of a bitch!" These words brought a scarlet blush to Miss Lin's cheeks, but Mr. Lin showed no change of expression. All the shops were selling Japanese merchandise. Moreover, after spending a few hundred dollars, the merchants had received special authorizations from the Guomindang chieftains, saying, "The goods may be sold after removing the Japanese markings." All the merchandise in Mr. Lin's shop had been transformed into "native goods." His customers, too, would call them "native goods," then take up their packages and leave.

Because of the war in Shanghai, the whole town had lost all interest in business, but Mr. Lin was busy pondering his affairs. Unwilling

「哦,那麼,有人說栗市快班強盜搶麼?」

林小姐搖頭,就像撲火的燈蛾似的撲向外面去了。林先生遲疑了一會兒,站在那蝴蝶門邊抓頭皮。林大娘在裏面打呃,又是喃喃地禱告:「菩薩保祐,炸彈不要落到我們頭上來!」林先生轉身再到鋪子裏,卻見女兒和兩個店員正在談得很熱鬧。對門生泰雜貨店裏的老闆金老虎也站在櫃台外邊指手劃腳地講談。上海打仗,東洋飛機擲炸彈燒了閘北,上海已經罷市,全都證實了。強盜搶快班船麼?沒有聽人說起過呀!栗市快班麼?早已到了,一路平安。金老虎看見那快班船上的夥計剛剛背着兩個蒲包走過的。林先生心裏鬆一口氣,知道壽生今天又沒回來,但也知道好好兒的沒有逢到強盜搶。

現在是滿街都在議論上海的戰事了。小夥計們夾在鬧裏罵「東洋烏龜!」竟也有人當街大呼:「再買東洋貨就是忘八!」林小姐聽着,臉上就飛紅了一大片。林先生卻還不動神色。大家都賣東洋貨,並且大家花了幾百塊錢以後,都已經奉着特許:「只要把東洋商標撕去了就行。」他現在滿店的貨物都已經稱為「國貨」,買主們也都是「國貨,國貨」地說着,就拿走了。在此滿街人人為了上海的戰事而沒有心思想到生意的時候,林先生始終在籌慮他的正事。他還是不肯花

to borrow from the local bank at exorbitant interest, he sought out the collector from the Shanghai wholesale house, to plead with him as a friend for a delay of another day or two. Shousheng would be back tomorrow before dark at the latest, said Mr. Lin. Then he would pay in full.

"My dear Mr. Lin, you're an intelligent man. How can you talk like that? They're fighting in Shanghai. Train service may be cut off tomorrow or the day after. I only wish I could start back tonight! How can I wait a day or two? Please, settle your account today so that I can leave the first thing tomorrow morning. I'm not my own boss. Please have some consideration for me!"

The Shanghai collector was uncompromisingly firm in his refusal. Mr. Lin saw that it was hopeless; he had no choice but to bear the pain and seek a loan from the local banker. He was worried that "Old Miser" knew of his sore need and would take advantage of the situation to boost the interest rate. From the minute he started speaking to the bank manager, Mr. Lin could feel that the atmosphere was all wrong. The tubercular old man said nothing when Mr. Lin finished his plea, but continued puffing on his antique water-pipe. After the whole packet of tobacco was consumed, the manager finally spoke.

"I can't do it," he said slowly. "The Japanese have begun fighting, business in Shanghai is at a standstill, the banks have all closed down — who knows when things will be set right again! Cut off from Shanghai, my bank is like a crab without legs. With exchange of remittances stopped, I couldn't do business even with a better client than you. I'm sorry. I'd love to help you but my hands are tied!"

Mr. Lin lingered. He thought the tubercular manager was putting on an act in preparation for demanding higher interest. Just as Mr. Lin was about to play along by renewing his pleas, he was surprised to hear the manager press him a step farther.

重利去借莊款,他去和上海號家的收賬客人情商,請他再多等這麼一天兩天。他的壽生極遲明天傍晚總該會到。

「林老闆,你也是明白人,怎麼說出這種話來呀!現在上海開了火,說不定明後天火車就不通,我是巴不得今晚上就動身呢!怎麼再等一兩天?請你今天把賬款繳清,明天一早我好走。我也是吃人家的飯,請你照顧照顧罷!」

上海客人毫無通融地拒絕了林先生的情商。林先生看來是無可商量了,只好忍痛去到恆源錢莊上商借。他還恐怕那「錢獅猻」知道他是急用,要趁火打劫,高抬利息。誰知錢莊經理的口氣卻完全不對了。那癆病鬼經理聽完了林先生的申請,並沒作答,只管捧着他那老古董的水煙筒卜落落卜落落的呼,直到燒完一根紙吹,這才慢吞吞地說:

「不行了!東洋兵開仗,上海罷市,銀行錢莊都封關,知道他們幾時弄得好!上海這路一斷,敝莊就成了沒腳蟹,匯劃不通,比尊處再好的戶頭也只好不做了。對不起,實在愛莫能助!」

林先生呆了一呆,還總以為這癆病鬼經理故意刁難,無非是為提高利息作地步,正想結結實實說幾句懇求的話,卻不料那經理又逼進一步道:

"Our employer has given us instructions. He has heard that the situation will probably get worse. He wants us to tighten up. Your shop originally owed us five hundred; on the twentysecond, you borrowed another hundred — altogether six hundred, due to be settled before New Year. We've been doing business together a long time, so I'm tipping you off. We want to avoid a lot off talk and embarrassment at the last minute."

"Oh — but our little shop is having a hard time," blurted the dumbfounded Mr. Lin. "I'll have to see how we do with our collections."

"Ho! Why be so modest! The last few days your business hasn't been like the others! What's so difficult about paying a mere six hundred dollars? I'm letting you know today, old brother. I'm looking forward to your settling your debt so that I can clear myself with my employer."

The tubercular manager spoke coldly. He stood up. Chilled, Mr. Lin could see that the situation was beyond repair. All he could do was to take a grip on himself and walk out of the bank. At last he understood that the fighting in distant Shanghai would influence his little shop too. It certainly was going to be hard to get through this New Year: The Shanghai collector was pressing him for money; the bank wouldn't wait until after the New Year; Shousheng still hadn't come back and there was no telling how he was getting on. So far as Mr. Lin's outstanding accounts in town were concerned, last year he had only collected eighty per cent. From the looks of things, this year there was no guarantee of even that much. Only one road seemed open to Mr. Lin: "Business Temporarily Closed — Balancing Books!" And this was equivalent to bankruptcy. There hadn't been any of his own money invested in the shop for a long time. The day the books were balanced and the creditors paid off, what would be left for him

「剛才敝東吩咐過，他得的信，這次的亂子恐怕要鬧大，叫我們收緊盤子！尊處原欠五百，二十二那天，又是一百，總共是六百，年關前總得掃數歸清；我們也算是老主顧，今天先透一個信，免得臨時多費口舌，大家面子上難為情。」

「哦——可是小店裏也實在為難。要看賬頭收得怎樣。」

林先生呆了半晌，這才吶出這兩句話。

「嘿！何必客氣！寶號裏這幾天來的生意比眾不同，區區六百塊錢，還為難麼？今天是同老兄說明白了，總望掃數歸清，我在敝東跟前好交代。」

癆病鬼經理冷冷地說，站起來了。林先生冷了半截身子，瞧情形是萬難挽回，只好硬着頭皮走出了那家錢莊。他此時這才明白原來遠在上海的打仗也要影響到他的小鋪子了。今年的年關當真是難過：上海的收賬客人立逼着要錢，恆源裏不許宕過年，壽生還沒回來，知道他怎樣了，鎮上的賬頭，去年只收起八成，今年瞧來連八成都捏不穩——橫在他前面的路，只是一條：「暫停營業，清理賬目！」而這條路也就等於破產，他這鋪子裏早已沒有自己的資本，一

probably wouldn't be enough to stand between his family and nakedness!

The more he thought, the worse Mr. Lin felt. Crossing the bridge, he looked at the turbid water below. He was almost tempted to jump and end it all. Then a man hailed him from behind.

"Mr. Lin, is it true there's a war on in Shanghai? I hear that a bunch of soldiers just set up outside the town's east gate and asked the Merchants Guild for a 'loan.' They wanted twenty thousand right off the bat. The Merchants Guild is holding a meeting about it now!"

Mr. Lin hurriedly turned around. The speaker was Old Chen who had two hundred dollars loaned to the shop — another of Mr. Lin's creditors.

"Oh — " retorted Mr. Lin with a shiver. Quickly he crossed the bridge and ran home.

IV

For dinner that evening, beside the usual one meat dish and two vegetable dishes, Mrs. Lin had bought a favourite of Mr. Lin's — a platter of stewed pork. In addition, there was a pint of yellow wine. A smile never left Miss Lin's face, for business in the shop was good, her new silk dress was finished, and because they were fighting back against the Japanese in Shanghai. Mrs. Lin's hiccups were especially sparse — about one every ten minutes.

Only Mr. Lin was sunk in gloom. Moodily drinking his wine, he looked at his daughter, and looked at his wife. Several times he con-

旦清理，剩給他的，光景只有一家三口三個光身子！

林先生愈想愈仄，走過那座望仙橋時，他看着橋下的渾水，幾乎想縱身一跳完事。可是有一個人在背後喚他道：

「林先生，上海打仗了，是真的罷？聽說東柵外剛剛調來了一支兵，到商會裏要借餉，開口就是二萬，商會裏正在開會呢！」

林先生急回過臉去看，原來正是那位存有兩百塊錢在他鋪子裏的陳老七，也是林先生的一位債主。

「哦──」

林先生打一個冷噤，只回答了這一聲，就趕快下橋，一口氣跑回家去。

四

這晚上的夜飯，林大娘在家常的一葷二素以外，特又添了一個碟子，是到八仙樓買來的紅燜肉，林先生心愛的東西。另外又有一斤黃酒。林小姐笑不離口，為的鋪子裏生意好，為的大綢新旗袍已經做成，也為的上海竟然開火，打東洋人。林大娘打呃的次數更加少了，差不多十分鐘只來一回。

只有林先生心裏發悶到要死。他喝着悶酒，看看女兒，又看看老婆，幾次想把那炸彈似的惡消息宣布，然而終於沒有那樣的勇

sidered dropping the bad news in their midst like a bombshell, but he didn't have that kind of courage. Moreover, he still hadn't given up hope, he still wanted to struggle; at least he wanted to conceal his failure to make ends meet.

And so when the Merchants Guild passed a resolution to pay the soldiers five thousand dollars and asked Mr. Lin to contribute twenty, he consented without a moment's hesitation. He decided not to tell his wife and daughter the true state of affairs until the last possible minute. The way he calculated it was this: He would collect eighty per cent of the debts due him, he would pay eighty per cent of the money he owed. Anyhow, he had the excuse that there was fighting in Shanghai, that remittances couldn't be sent. The difficulty was that there was a difference of about six hundred dollars between what people owed him and what he had to pay to others. He would have to take drastic measures and cut prices heavily. The idea was to scrape together some money to meet the present problem, then he would see. Who could think of the future in times like these? If he could get by now, that would be enough.

That was how he made his plans. With the added potency of the pint of yellow wine, Mr. Lin slept soundly all night, without even the suggestion of a bad dream.

It was already six thirty when Mr. Lin awoke the next morning. The sky was overcast and he was rather dizzy. He gulped down two bowls of rice gruel and hurried to the shop. The first thing to greet his eye was the Shanghai collector, sitting with a stern face, waiting for his "answer." But what shocked Mr. Lin particularly was the shop across the street. They too had pasted red and green strips all over their windows; they too were having a "Big Sale 10% Discount"! Mr. Lin's perfect plan of the night before was completely snowed under by those red and green streamers of his competitor.

氣。並且他還不曾絕望，還想掙扎，至少是還想掩飾他的兩下裏碰不到頭。所以當商會裏議決了答應借餉五千並且要林先生攤認二十元的時候，他毫不推托，就答應下來了。他決定非到最後五分鐘不讓老婆和女兒知道那家道困難的真實情形。他的劃算是這樣的：人家欠他的賬收一個八成罷，他還人家的賬也是個八成，——反正可以藉口上海打仗，錢莊不通；為難的是人欠我欠之間尚差六百光景，那只有用剜肉補瘡的方法拚命放盤賣賤貨，且撈幾個錢來渡過了眼前再說。這年頭兒，誰能夠顧到將來呢？眼前得過且過。

是這麼想定了方法，又加上那一斤黃酒的力量，林先生倒酣睡了一夜，惡夢也沒有半個。

第二天早上，林先生醒來時已經是六點半鐘，天色很陰沉。林先生覺得有點頭暈。他匆匆忙忙吞進兩碗稀飯，就到鋪子裏，一眼就看見那位上海客人板起了臉孔在那裏坐守「回話」。而尤其叫林先生猛吃一驚的，是斜對門的裕昌祥也貼起紅紅綠綠的紙條，也在那裏「大放盤照碼九折」了！林先生昨夜想好的「如意算盤」立刻被斜對門那些紅綠紙條衝一個搖搖不定。

"What kind of a joke is this, Mr. Lin? Last night you didn't give a reply. That boat leaves here at eight o'clock and I have to make connections with the train. I simply must catch that eight o'clock boat! Please hurry — "said the Shanghai collector impatiently. He brought his clenched fist down on the table.

Mr. Lin apologized and begged his forgiveness. Truly, it was all because of the fighting in Shanghai and not being able to send remittances. After all, they had been doing business for many years. Mr. Lin pleaded for a little special consideration.

"Then am I to go back empty-handed?"

"Why, why, certainly not. When Shousheng returns, I'll give you as much as he brings. I'm not a man if I keep so much as half a dollar!" Mr. Lin's voice trembled. With an effort he held back the tears that brimmed to his eyes.

There was no more to be said: the Shanghai collector stopped his grumbling. But he remained firmly seated where he was. Mr. Lin was nearly out of his wits with anxiety. His heart thumped erratically. Although he had been having a hard time the past few years, he had been able to keep up a front. Now there was a collector sitting in his shop for all the world to see. If word of this thing spread, Mr. Lin's credit would be ruined. He had plenty of creditors. Suppose they all decided to follow suit? His shop might just as well close down immediately. In desperation, several times he invited the Shanghai gentleman to wait in the back room where it was more comfortable, but the latter refused.

An icy rain began to fall. The street was cold and deserted. Never had it appeared so mournful at New Year's time. Signboards creaked and clattered in the grip of a north wind. The icy rain seemed like to turn into snow. In the shops that lined the street, salesmen leaning on the counters looked up blankly.

「林老闆，你真是開玩笑！昨晚上不給我回音。輪船是八點鐘開，我還得轉乘火車，八點鐘這班船我是非走不行！請你快點──」

上海客人不耐煩地說，把一個拳頭在桌子上一放。林先生只有陪不是，請他原諒，實在是因為上海打仗錢莊不通，彼此是多年的老主顧，務請格外看承。

「那麼叫我空手回去麼？」

「這，這，斷乎不會。我們的壽生一回來，有多少付多少，我要是藏落半個錢，不是人！」

林先生顫着聲音說，努力忍住了滾到眼眶邊的眼淚。

話是說到盡頭了，上海客人只好不再嚕囌，可是他坐在那裏不肯走。林先生急得什麼似的，心是卜卜地亂跳。近年他雖然萬分拮据，面子上可還遮得過；現在擺一個人在鋪子裏坐守，這件事要是傳揚開去，他的信用可就完了，他的債戶還多着呢，萬一群起效尤，他這鋪子只好立刻關門。他在沒有辦法中想辦法。幾次請這位討賬客人到內宅去坐，然而討賬客人不肯。

天又索索地下起凍雨來了。一條街上冷清清地簡直沒有人行。自有這條街以來，從沒見過這樣蕭索的臘尾歲盡。朔風吹着那些招牌，嚓嚓地響。漸漸地凍雨又有變成雪花的模樣。沿街店鋪裏的夥計們靠在櫃台上仰起了臉發怔。

Occasionally, Mr. Lin and the collector from Shanghai exchanged a few desultory words. Miss Lin suddenly emerged through the swinging doors and stood at the front window watching the cold hissing rain. From the back room, the sound of Mrs. Lin's hiccups steadily gathered intensity. While trying to be pleasant to their visitor, Mr. Lin looked at his daughter and listened to his wife's hiccups, and a wave of depression rose in his breast. He thought how all his life he had never known any prosperity, nor could he imagine who was responsible for his being reduced to such dire straits today.

The Shanghai collector seemed to have calmed down somewhat. "Mr. Lin," he said abruptly, in a sincere tone, "you're a good man. You don't go in for loose living, you're obliging and honest in your business practices. Twenty years ago, you would have gotten rich. But things are different today. Taxes are high, expenses are heavy, business is slow — it's an accomplishment just to get along."

Mr. Lin sighed and smiled in wry modesty.

After a pause, the Shanghai collector continued, "This year the market in this town was a little worse than last, wasn't it? Places in the interior like this depend on the people from the countryside for business, but the peasants are too poor. There's really no solution.... Oh, it's nine o'clock! Why hasn't your collection clerk come back yet? Is he reliable?"

Mr. Lin's heart gave a leap. For the moment, he couldn't answer. Although Shousheng had been his salesman for seven or eight years and had never made a slip, still, there was no absolute guarantee! And besides he was overdue. The Shanghai collector laughed to see Mr. Lin's doubtful expression, but his laugh had an odd ring to it.

At the window, Miss Lin whirled and cried urgently, "Papa, Shousheng is back! He's covered with mud!"

　　林先生和那位收賬客人有一句沒一句的閒談着。林小姐忽然走出蝴蝶門來站在街邊看那索索的凍雨。從蝴蝶門後送來的林大娘的呃呃的聲音又漸漸兒加勤。林先生嘴裏應酬着，一邊看看女兒，又聽聽老婆的打呃，心裏一陣一陣酸上來，想起他的一生簡直毫沒幸福，然而又不知道坑害他到這地步的，究竟是誰。那位上海客人似乎氣平了一些了，忽然很懇切地說：

　　「林老闆，你是個好人。一點嗜好都沒有，做生意很巴結認真。放在二十年前，你怕不發財麼？可是現今時勢不同，捐稅重，開銷大，生意又清；混得過也還是你的本事。」

　　林先生嘆一口氣苦笑着，算是謙遜。

　　上海客人頓了一頓，又接着說下去：

　　「貴鎮上的市面今年又比上年差些，是不是？內地全靠鄉莊生意，鄉下人太窮，真是沒有法子，——呀，九點鐘了！怎麼你們的收賬夥計還沒來呢？這個人靠得住麼？」

　　林先生心裏一跳，暫時回答不出來。雖然是七八年的老夥計，一向沒有出過岔子，但誰能保到底呢！而況又是過期不見回來。上海客人看着林先生那遲疑的神氣，就笑；那笑聲有幾分異樣。忽然那邊林小姐轉臉對林先生急促地叫道：

　　「爸爸，壽生回來了！一身泥！」

Her voice had a peculiar sound too. Mr. Lin jumped up, both alarmed and happy. He wanted to run out and look, but he was so excited that his legs were weak. By then Shousheng had already entered, truly covered with mud. The clerk sat down, panting for breath, unable to say a word. The situation looked bad. Frightened out of his wits, Mr. Lin was speechless too. The Shanghai collector frowned. After a while, Shousheng managed to gasp:

"Very dangerous! They nearly got me!"

"Then the boat was robbed?" the agitated Mr. Lin took a grip on himself and blurted.

"There wasn't any robbing. They were grabbing coolies for the army. I couldn't make the boat yesterday afternoon; I got a sampan this morning. After we sailed, we heard they were waiting at this end to grab the boat, so we came to port further down the river. When we got ashore, before we had come half a *li*, we bumped into an army pressgang. They grabbed the clerk from the clothing shop, but I ran fast and came back by a short cut. Damn it! It was a close call!"

Shousheng lifted his jacket as he talked and pulled from his money belt a cloth-bound packet which he handed to Mr. Lin.

"It's all here," he said. "That Huang Shop in Lishi is rotten. We have to be careful of customers like that next year.... I'll come back after I have a wash and change my clothes."

Mr. Lin's face lit up as he squeezed the packet. He carried it over to the cashier's cage and unbound the cloth wrapping. First he added up the money due on the list of debtors, then he counted what had been collected. There were eleven silver dollars, two hundred dimes, four hundred and twenty dollars in banknotes, and two bank demand drafts — for the equivalent of fifty and sixty-five taels of silver respectively, at the official rate. If he turned the whole lot over to the

顯然林小姐的叫聲也是異樣的，林先生跳起來，又驚又喜，着急的想跑到櫃台前去看，可是心慌了，兩腿發軟。這時壽生已經跑了進來，當真是一身泥，氣喘喘地坐下了，説不出話來。林先生估量那情形不對，嚇得沒有主意，也不開口。上海客人在旁邊皺眉頭。過了一會兒，壽生方才喘着氣説：

「好險呀！差一些兒被他們抓住了。」

「到底是強盜搶了快班船麼？」

林先生驚極，心一橫，倒逼出話來了。

「不是強盜。是兵隊拉夫呀！昨天下午趕不上趁快班。今天一早趁航船，哪裏知道航船聽得這裏要捉船，就停在東柵外了。我上岸走不到半里路，就碰到拉夫。西面寶祥衣莊的阿毛被他們拉去了。我跑得快，抄小路逃了回來。他媽的，性命交關！」

壽生一面説，一面撩起衣服，從肚兜裏掏出一個手巾包來遞給了林先生，又説道：

「都在這裏了。栗市的那家黃茂記很可惡，這種戶頭，我們明年要留心！——我去洗一個臉，換件衣服再來。」

林先生接了那手巾包，捏一把；臉上有些笑容了。他到賬台裏打開那手巾包來。先看一看那張「清單」，打了一會兒算盤，然後點檢銀錢數目：是大洋十一元，小洋二百角，鈔票四百二十元，外加即期莊票兩張，一張是規元五十兩，又一張是規元六十五兩。這全

Shanghai collector, it would still be more than a hundred dollars short of what he owed the wholesale house.

Deep in contemplation, Mr. Lin glanced several times out of the corner of his eye at the Shanghai collector who was silently smoking a cigarette. At last he sighed, and as though cutting off a piece of his living flesh, placed the two bank drafts and four hundred dollars in cash before the man from Shanghai. Then Mr. Lin spoke for a long time until he managed to extract a nod from the latter and the words "all right."

But when the collector looked twice at the bank drafts, he said with a smile, "Sorry to trouble you, Mr. Lin. Please get them cashed for me first."

"Certainly, certainly," Mr. Lin hastened to reply. He quickly affixed his shop's seal to the back of the drafts and dispatched one of his salesmen to cash them at the local bank. In a little while, the salesman came back empty-handed. The bank had accepted the drafts but refused to pay for them, saying they would be credited against Mr. Lin's debt. Though it was snowing heavily now, Mr. Lin rushed over to the bank without an umbrella to plead in person. But his efforts were in vain.

"Well, what about it?" demanded the Shanghai collector impatiently as Mr. Lin returned to the shop, his face anguished.

Mr. Lin seemed ready to weep. There was nothing he could say; he could only sigh. Except to beg the collector for more leniency, what else could he do? Shousheng came out and added his pleas to Mr. Lin's. He vowed that they would send the remaining two hundred dollars to Shanghai by the tenth of the new year. Mr. Lin was an old customer who had always paid his debts promptly without a word, said Shousheng. This thing today was really unexpected. But that was

部付給上海客人，照賬算也還差一百多元。林先生凝神想了半晌，斜眼偷看了坐在那裏吸煙的上海客人幾次，方才嘆一口氣，割肉似的拿起那兩張莊票和四百元鈔票捧到上海客人跟前，又說了許多話，方才得到上海客人點一下頭，說一聲「對啦」。

但是上海客人把莊票看了兩遍，忽又笑着說道：

「對不起，林老闆，這莊票，費神兌了鈔票給我罷！」

「可以，可以。」

林先生連忙回答，慌忙在莊票後面蓋了本店的書朿圖章，派一個夥計到恆源莊去取現，並且叮囑了要鈔票。又過了半晌，夥計卻是空手回來。恆源莊把票子收了，但不肯付錢；據說是扣抵了林先生的欠款。天是在當真下雪了，林先生也沒張傘，冒雪到恆源莊去親自交涉，結果是徒然。

「林老闆，怎樣了呢？」

看見林先生苦着臉跑回來，那上海客人不耐煩地問了。

林先生幾乎想哭出來，沒有話回答，只是嘆氣。除了央求那上海客人再通融，還有什麼別的辦法？壽生也來了，幫着林先生說。他們賭咒：下欠的二百多元，趕明年初十邊一定匯到上海。是老主

the situation; they couldn't help themselves. It wasn't that they were stalling.

The Shanghai collector was adamant. Painfully, Mr. Lin brought out the fifty dollars he had taken in during the past few days and handed it over to make up a total payment of four hundred and fifty dollars. Only then did that headache of a Shanghai collector depart.

By that time, it was eleven in the morning. Snowflakes were still drifting down from the sky. Not even half a customer was in sight. Mr. Lin brooded a while, then discussed with Shousheng means to be used in collecting outstanding bills in town. Both men were frowning; neither of them had any particular confidence that much of the six hundred dollars due from town customers could be collected. Shousheng bent close to Mr. Lin's ear and whispered:

"I hear that the big shop at the south gate and the one at the west gate are both shaky. Both of them owe us money — about three hundred dollars altogether. We better take precautions with these two accounts. If they fold up before we can collect, it won't be so funny!"

Mr. Lin paled; his lips trembled a little. Then, Shousheng pitched his voice lower still, and mumbled a bit of even more shocking news.

"There's another nasty rumour — about us. They're sure to have heard it at the bank. That's why they're pressing us so hard. The Shanghai collector probably got wind of it too. Who can be trying to make trouble for us? The shop across the street?"

Shousheng pointed with his pursed lips in the direction of the suspect, and Mr. Lin's eyes swung to follow the indicator. His heart skipping unevenly, his face mournful, Mr. Lin was unable to speak for some time. He had the numb and aching feeling that this time he

顧了，向來三節清賬，從沒半句話，今兒實在是意外之變，大局如此，沒有辦法，非是他們刁賴。

然而不添一些，到底是不行的。林先生忍痛又把這幾天內賣得的現款湊成了五十元，算是總共付了四百五十元，這才把那位叫人頭痛的上海收賬客人送走了。

此時已有十一點了，天還是飄飄揚揚落着雪。買客沒有半個。林先生納悶了一會兒，和壽生商量本街的賬頭怎樣去收討。兩個人的眉頭都皺緊了，都覺得本鎮的六百多元賬頭收起來真沒有把握。壽生挨着林先生的耳朵悄悄地說道：

「聽說南柵的聚隆，西柵的和源，都不穩呢！這兩處欠我們的，就有三百光景，這兩筆倒賬要預先防着，吃下了，可不是玩的！」

林先生臉色變了，嘴唇有點抖。不料壽生把聲音再放低些，支支吾吾地說出了更駭人的消息來：

「還有，還有討厭的謠言，是說我們這裏了。恆源莊上一定聽得了這些風聲，這才對我們逼得那麼急，說不定上海的收賬客人也有點曉得——只是，誰和我們作對呢？難道就是斜對門麼？」

壽生說着，就把嘴向裕昌祥那邊呶了一呶。林先生的眼光跟着壽生的嘴也向那邊瞥了一下，心裏直是亂跳，哭喪着臉，好半天說不出話來。他的又麻又痛的心裏感到這一次他準是毀了！——不毀

was definitely finished! If he weren't ruined it would be a miracle: The Guomindang chieftains were putting the squeeze on him; the bank was pressing him; his fellow shopkeepers were stabbing him in the back; a couple of his biggest debtors were going to default. Nobody could stand up under this kind of buffeting. But why was he fated to get such a dirty deal? Ever since he inherited the little shop from his father, he had never dared to be wasteful. He had been so obliging; he never hurt a soul, never schemed against anyone. His father and grandfather had been the same, yet all he was reaping was bitterness!

"Never mind. Let them spread their rumours. You don't have to worry," Shousheng tried to comfort Mr. Lin, though he couldn't help sighing himself. "There are always rumours in lean years. They say in this town nine out of ten shops won't be able to pay up their debts before the year is out. Times are bad, the market is dead as a doornail. Usually strong shops are hard up this year. We're not the only one having rough going! When the sky tumbles everyone gets crushed. The Merchants Guild has to think of a way out. All the shops can't be collapsing; that would make the market even less like a market."

The snowfall was becoming heavier; it was sticking to the ground now. Occasionally, a dog would slink by, shivering, its tail between its legs. It might stop and shake itself violently to dislodge the snow thickly matting its fur. Then, with tail drooping again, the dog would go on its way. Never in its history had this street witnessed so frigid and desolate a New Year season! And just at this time, in distant Shanghai, Japanese heavy artillery was savagely pounding that prosperous metropolis of trade.

才是作怪：黨老爺敲詐他，錢莊壓逼他，同業又中傷他，而又要吃倒賬，憑誰也受不了這樣重重的磨折罷？而究竟為了什麼他應該活受罪呀！他，從父親手裏繼承下這小小的鋪子，從沒敢浪費；他，做生意多麼巴結；他，沒有害過人，沒有起過歹心；就是他的祖上，也沒害過人，做過歹事呀！然而他直如此命苦！

「不過，師傅，隨他們去造謠罷，你不要發急。荒年傳亂話，聽說是鎮上的店鋪十家有九家沒法過年關。時勢不好，市面清得不成話，素來硬朗的鋪子今年都打饑荒，也不是我們一家困難！天塌壓大家，商會裏總得議個辦法出來；總不能大家一齊拖倒，弄得市面更加不像市面。」

看見林先生急苦了，壽生姑且安慰着，忍不住也嘆了一口氣。

雪是愈下愈密了，街上已經見白。偶爾有一條狗垂着尾巴走過，抖一抖身體，搖落了厚積在毛上的那些雪，就又悄悄地夾着尾巴走了。自從有這條街以來，從沒見過這樣冷落淒涼的年關！而此時，遠在上海，日本軍的重炮正在發狂地轟毀那邊繁盛的市廛。

V

It was a gloomy New Year, but finally it was passed. In town, twenty-eight big and little shops folded up, including a "credit A-1" silk shop. The two stores that owed Mr. Lin three hundred dollars closed down too. The last day of the year, Shousheng had gone to them and plagued them for hours, but all he could extract was a total of twenty dollars. He heard that afterwards no other collector got so much as a penny out of them; the owners of the two shops hid themselves and couldn't be found. Thanks to the intervention of the head of the Merchants Guild, it wasn't necessary for Mr. Lin to hide. But he had to guarantee to wipe off his debt of four hundred dollars to the bank before the fifteenth of the first month, and he had to consent to very harsh terms: The bank would send a representative to "guard" all cash taken in starting from resumption of business on the fifth; eighty per cent of all money collected would go to the bank until Mr. Lin's debt to them was paid.

During the New Year holidays, Mr. Lin's house was like an ice box. Mr. Lin heaved sigh after sigh. Mrs. Lin's hiccups were like a string of firecrackers. Miss Lin, although she neither hiccuped nor sighed, moped around in the dazed condition of one who has suffered from years of jaundice. Her new silk dress had already gone to the only pawnshop in town to raise money for the maid's wages. An apprentice had taken it there at seven in the morning; it was after nine when he finally squeezed his way out of the crowd with two dollars in his hand. Afterwards, the pawnshop refused to do any more business that day. Two dollars! That was the highest price they would give for any article, no matter how much you had paid for it originally!

五

　　淒涼的年關，終於也過去了。鎮上的大小鋪子倒閉了二十八家。內中有一家「信用素著」的綢莊。欠了林先生三百元貨賬的聚隆與和源也畢竟倒了。大年夜的白天，壽生到那兩個鋪子裏磨了半天，也只拿了二十多塊來；這以後，就聽說沒有一個收賬員拿到半文錢，兩家鋪子的老闆都躲得不見面了。林先生自己呢，多虧商會長一力斡旋，還無須往鄉下躲，然而欠下恆源錢莊的四百多元非要正月十五以前還清不可；並且又訂了苛刻的條件：從正月初五開市那天起，恆源就要派人到林先生鋪子裏「守提」，賣得的錢，八成歸恆源扣賬。

　　新年那四天，林先生家裏就像一個冰窖。林先生常常嘆氣，林大娘的打呃像連珠炮。林小姐雖然不打呃，也不嘆氣，但是呆呆地好像害了多年的黃病。她那件大綢新旗袍，為的要付吳媽的工錢，已經上了當鋪；小學徒從清早七點鐘就去那家唯一的當鋪門前守候，直到九點鐘方才從人堆裏拿了兩塊錢擠出來。以後，當鋪就止當了。兩塊錢！這已是最高價。隨你值多少錢的貴重衣飾，也只

This was called "two dollar ceiling." When a peasant, steeling himself against the cold, would peel off a cotton-padded jacket and hand it across the counter, the pawnshop clerk would raise it up, give it a shake, then fling it back with an angry "We don't want it!"

Since New Year's Day, the weather had been beautiful and clear. The big temple courtyard, as was the custom, was crowded with the stalls of itinerant pedlars and the paraphernalia of acrobats and jugglers. People lingered before the stalls, patted their empty money belts, and reluctantly walked on. Children dragged at their mothers' clothing, refusing to leave the stall where fireworks were on sale, until Mama was forced to give the little offender a hard slap. The pedlars, who had come specially to cash in on the usual New Year's bazaar trade, didn't even make enough to pay for their food. They couldn't pay their rent at the local inn and quarrelled with the innkeeper every day.

Only the acrobatic troupe earned the large sum of eight dollars. It had been hired by the Guomindang chieftains to add to the atmosphere of "peace and normalcy."

On the evening of the fourth, Mr. Lin, who had with some difficulty managed to raise three dollars, gave the usual spread for his employees at which they all discussed the strategy for the morrow's re-opening of business. The prospects were already terribly clear to Mr. Lin: If they re-opened, they were sure to operate at a loss; if they didn't re-open, he and his family would be entirely without resources. Moreover, people still owed him four hundred dollars, the collection of which would be even more difficult, if he closed down. The only way out was to cut expenses. But taxes and levies for the soldiers were inescapable; there was even less chance of his avoiding being "squeezed." Fire a couple of salesmen? He only had three. Shousheng was his righthand man; the other two were poor devils; besides he

能當得兩塊呢！叫做「兩塊錢封門」。鄉下人忍着冷剝下身上的棉襖遞上櫃台去，那當鋪裏的夥計拿起來抖了一抖，就直丟出去，怒聲喊道：「不當！」

元旦起，是大好的晴天。關帝廟前那空場上，照例來了跑江湖趕新年生意的攤販和變把戲的雜耍。人們在那些攤子面前懶懶地拖着腿走，兩手捫着空的腰包，就又懶懶地走開了。孩子們拉住了娘的衣角，賴在花炮攤前不肯走，娘就給他一個老大的耳光。那些特來趕新年的攤販們連伙食都開銷不了，白賴在「安商客寓」裏，天天和客寓主人吵鬧。

只有那班變把戲的出了八塊錢的大生意，黨老爺們喚他們去點綴了一番「昇平氣象」。

初四那天晚上，林先生勉強籌措了三塊錢，辦一席酒請鋪子裏的「相好」吃照例的「五路酒」，商量明天開市的辦法。林先生早就籌思過熟透：這鋪子開下去呢，眼見得是虧本的生意，不開呢，他一家三口兒簡直沒有生計，而且到底人家欠他的貨賬還有四五百，他一關門更難討取；惟一的辦法是減省開支，但捐稅派餉是逃不了的，「敲詐」尤其無法躲避，裁去一兩個店員罷，本來他只有三個夥計，壽生是左右手，其餘的兩位也是怪可憐見的，況且辭歇了到底

really needed them to wait on the customers. He couldn't save any more at home. They had already let the maid go. He felt the only thing to do was to plunge on. Perhaps, when the peasants, with Buddha's blessing, earned money from their spring raw silk sales, he still might make up his loss.

But the greatest problem in resuming business was that he was short of merchandise. Without money to remit to Shanghai, he couldn't replenish his stock. The fighting in Shanghai was getting worse. There was no use in hoping for getting anything on credit. Sell his reserve? The shop was long since actually cleaned out. The underwear boxes on the shelves were empty; they were used only for show. All that was left were things like wash-basins and towels. But he had plenty of those.

Gloomily, the feasters sipped their wine. For all their perplexed reflection, no one could offer any solution to the problem. They talked of generalities for a while. Then suddenly A Si, one of the salesmen, said:

"The world is going to hell. People live worse than dogs! They say Zhabei was completely burned out. A couple of hundred thousand people had to flee, leaving all their belongings behind. There wasn't any fire in the Hongkou section, but everybody ran away. The Japanese are very cruel. They wouldn't let them take any of their things with them. House rent in safe quarters in Shanghai has skyrocketed. All the refugees are running to the countryside. A bunch came to our town yesterday. They all look like decent people, and now they're homeless!"

Mr. Lin shook his head and sighed, but Shousheng, on hearing these words, was suddenly struck with a bright idea. He put down his chopsticks, then raised his wine cup and drained it in one swallow. He turned to Mr. Lin with a grin.

也不夠招呼生意；家裏呢，也無可再省，吳媽早已辭歇。他覺得只有硬着頭皮做下去，或者靠菩薩的保祐，鄉下人春蠶熟；他的虧空還可以補救。

但要開市，最大的困難是缺乏貨品。沒有現錢寄到上海去，就拿不到貨。上海打得更厲害了，賒賬是休轉這念頭。賣底貨罷，他店裏早已淘空，架子上那些裝衛生衣的紙盒就是空的，不過擺在那裏裝幌子。他鋪子裏就剩了些日用雜貨，臉盆毛巾之類，存底還厚。

大家喝了一會悶酒，抓腮挖耳地想不出好主意。後來談起閒天來，一個夥計忽然說。

「亂世年頭，人比不上狗！聽說上海閘北燒得精光，幾十萬人都只逃得一個光身子。虹口一帶呢，燒是還沒燒，人都逃光了，東洋人兇得很，不許搬東西。上海房錢漲起幾倍。逃出來的人都到鄉下來了，昨天鎮上就到了一批，看樣都是好好的人家，現在卻弄得無家可歸！」

林先生搖頭嘆氣。壽生聽了這話，猛的想起了一個好辦法；他放下了筷子，拿起酒杯來一口喝乾了，笑嘻嘻對林先生說道：

"Did you hear what A Si just said? That means our wash-basins, wash-cloths, soap, socks, tooth powder, tooth brushes, will sell fast. We can get rid of as many as we've got."

Mr. Lin stared. He didn't know what Shousheng was driving at.

"Look, this is a heaven-sent chance. The Shanghai refugees should have a little money, and they need the usual daily necessities, don't they? We ought to set up right away to handle this business!"

Shousheng poured himself another cup of wine, and drank, his face beaming. The two salesmen caught on, and they began to laugh. Only Mr. Lin was not entirely clear. He had been rather dulled by his recent adversity.

"Are you sure?" he asked, irresolutely. "Other shops have wash-cloths and wash-basins too — "

"But we're the only ones with any real reserve of that sort of stuff. They don't have even ten wash-basins across the street, and those are all seconds. We've got this piece of business right in the palm of our hand! Let's write a lot of ads and paste them up at the town's four gateways, any place in town where the refugees are staying — say, A Si, where *are* they living? We'll go put up our stickers there!"

"The ones with relatives here are living with their relatives. The rest have borrowed that empty building in the silk factory outside the west gate." A Si's face shone with satisfaction over the excellent result he had unwittingly produced.

At last, Mr. Lin had the whole picture. Happy, his spirits revived. He immediately drafted the wording of the advertisements, listing all the daily necessities which the shop had available for sale. There were over a dozen different commodities. In imitation of the big Shanghai stores, he adopted the "One Dollar Package" technique. For a dollar

「師傅，聽得阿四的話麼？我們那些臉盆，毛巾，肥皂，襪子，牙粉，牙刷，就可以如數銷清了。」

林先生瞪出了眼睛，不懂得壽生的意思。

「師傅，這是天大的機會。上海逃來的人，總還有幾個錢，他們總要買些日用的東西，是不是？這筆生意，我們趕快張羅。」

壽生接着又説，再篩出一杯酒來喝了，滿臉是喜氣。兩個夥計也省悟過來了，哈哈大笑。只有林先生還不很了然。近來的逆境已經把他變成糊塗。他惘然問道：

「你拿得穩麼？臉盆，毛巾，別家也有，──」

「師傅，你忘記了！臉盆毛巾一類的東西只有我們存底獨多！裕昌祥裏拿不出十隻臉盆，而且都是揀剩貨。這筆生意，逃不出我們的手掌心的了！我們趕快多寫幾張廣告到四柵去分貼，逃難人住的地方──噯，阿四，他們住在什麼地方？我們也要去貼廣告。」

「他們有親戚的住到親戚家裏去了，沒有的，還借住在西柵外繭廠的空房子。」

叫做阿四的夥計回答，臉上發亮，很得意自己的無意中立了大功。林先生這時也完全明白了。心裏一快樂，就又靈活起來，他馬上擬好了廣告的底稿，專揀店裏有的日用品開列上去，約莫也有十幾種。他又摹仿上海大商店賣「一元貨」的方法，把臉盆，毛巾，牙

the customer would get a wash-basin, a wash-cloth, a tooth brush and a box of tooth powder. "Big Dollar Sale!" screamed the ad in huge letters. Shousheng brought out the shop's remaining sheets of red and green paper and cut them into large strips. Then he took up his brush and started writing. The salesmen and the apprentices noisily collected the wash-basins, wash-cloths, tooth brushes and boxes of tooth powder, and arranged them into sets. There weren't enough hands for all the work. Mr. Lin called his daughter out to help with writing the ads and tying the packages. He also made up other kinds of combination packages — all of daily necessities.

That night, they were busy in the shop late and long. At dawn they had things pretty much in order. When the popping of firecrackers heralded the opening of business the next morning, the shop of the Lin family again had a new look. Their advertisements had already been pasted up all over town. Shousheng had personally attended to the silk factory outside the west gate. The ad with which he plastered the factory walls struck the eyes of the refugees, and they all crowded around to read it as if it were a news bulletin.

In the "inner sanctum" Mrs. Lin, too, rose very early. She lit incense before the porcelain image of the Goddess Guanyin and kowtowed for a considerable time, knocking her head resoundingly against the floor. She prayed for practically everything. About the only thing she omitted was a plea for more refugees to come to the town.

It all worked out fine, just as Shousheng had predicted. Mr. Lin's shop was the only one whose trade was brisk on the first business day after the New Year's holidays. By four in the afternoon, he had sold over one hundred dollars' worth of merchandise — the highest figure for a day ever reached in that town in the past ten years. His biggest seller was the "One Dollar Package," and it served as a leader to such items as umbrellas and rubber overshoes. Business, moreover, went

刷，牙粉配成一套賣一塊錢，廣告上就大書「大廉價一元貨」。店裏本來還有餘剩下的紅綠紙，壽生大張的裁好了，拿筆就寫。兩個夥計和學徒就亂烘烘地拿過臉盆，毛巾，牙刷，牙粉來裝配成一組。人手不夠，林先生叫女兒出來幫着寫，幫着紮配，另外又配出幾種「一元貨」，全是零星的日用必需品。

這一晚上，林家鋪子裏直忙到五更左右，方才大致就緒。第二天清早，開門鞭炮響過，排門開了，林家鋪子佈置得又是一新。漏夜趕起來的廣告早已漏夜分頭貼出去。西柵外繭廠一帶是壽生親自去佈置，哄動那些借住在繭廠裏的逃難人，都起來看，當做一件新聞。

「內宅」裏，林大娘也起了個五更，瓷觀音面前點了香，林大娘爬着磕了半天響頭。她什麼都禱告全了，就只差沒有禱告菩薩要上海的戰事再擴大再延長，好多來些逃難人。

一切都很順利，一切都不出壽生的預料。新正開市第一天就只林家鋪子生意很好，到下午四點多鐘，居然賣了一百多元，是這鎮上近十年來未有的新紀錄。銷售的大宗，果然是「一元貨」，然而洋傘橡皮雨鞋之類卻也帶起了銷路，並且那生意也做的乾脆有味。雖

smoothly, pleasantly. The refugees came from Shanghai, after all; they were used to the ways of the big city; they weren't as petty as the townspeople or peasants from the out-lying districts. When they bought something, they made up their minds quickly. They'd pick up a thing, look at it, then produce their money. There was none of this pawing through all the merchandise, no haggling over a few pennies.

When her daughter, all flushed and excited, rushed into the back room for a moment to report the good business, Mrs. Lin went to kowtow before the porcelain Guanyin again. If Shousheng weren't twice the girl's age, Mrs. Lin was thinking, wouldn't he make a good son-in-law! And it wasn't at all unlikely that Shousheng had half an eye on his employer's seventeen-year-old daughter, this girl whom he knew so well.

There was just one thing that spoiled Mr. Lin's happiness — completely disregarding his dignity, the local bank had sent its man to collect eighty per cent of the sales proceeds. And he didn't know who egged them on, but the three creditors of the shop, on the excuse that they "needed a little money to buy rice," all showed up to draw out some advance interest. Not only interest; they even wanted repayment of part of their loans too! But Mr. Lin also heard some good news — another batch of refugees had arrived in town.

For dinner that evening, Mr. Lin served two additional meat dishes, by way of reward to his employees. Everyone complimented Shousheng on his shrewdness. Although Mr. Lin was happy, he couldn't help thinking of how his three creditors had talked about being repaid their loans. It was unlucky to have such a thing happen at the beginning of the new year.

"What do they know!" said Shousheng angrily. "Somebody must have put them up to it!" He pointed with his lips at the shop across the street.

然是「逃難人」，卻畢竟住在上海，見過大場面，他們不像鄉下人或本鎮人那麼小格式，他們買東西很爽利，拿起貨來看了一眼，現錢交易，從不揀來揀去，也不硬要除零頭。

林大娘看見女兒興沖沖地跑進來誇說一回，就爬到瓷觀音面前磕了一回頭。她心裏還轉了這樣的念頭：要不是歲數相差得多，把壽生招做女婿倒也是好的！說不定在壽生那邊也時常用半隻眼睛望着這位廝熟的十七歲的「師妹」。

只有一點，使林先生掃興；恆源莊毫不顧面子地派人來提取了當天營業總數的八成。並且存戶朱三阿太，橋頭陳老七，還有張寡婦，不知聽了誰的慫恿，都藉了「要量米吃」的藉口，都來預支息金；不但支息金，還想拔提一點存款呢！但也有一個喜訊，聽説又到了一批逃難人。

晚餐時，林先生添了兩碟葷菜，酬勞他的店員。大家稱讚壽生能幹。林先生雖然高興，卻不能不惦念着朱三阿太等三位存戶要提存款的事情。大新年碰到這種事，總是不吉利。壽生憤然説：

「那三個懂得什麼呢！還不是有人從中挑撥！」

説着，壽生的嘴又向斜對門呶了一呶。林先生點頭。可是這三

Mr. Lin nodded. But whether the three creditors knew anything or not, it was going to be difficult to handle them. An old man and two widows. You couldn't be soft with them, but getting tough wouldn't either. Mr. Lin pondered for some time, and finally decided the best thing to do would be to ask the head of the Merchants Guild to speak to his three precious creditors. He asked Shousheng for his opinion. Shousheng heartily agreed.

When dinner was over, and Mr. Lin had added up his receipts for the day, he went to pay his respects to the head of the Merchants Guild. The latter expressed complete approval of Mr. Lin's idea. What's more, he commended Mr. Lin on the intelligent way in which he conducted his business. He said the shop was sure to stand firm, in fact it would improve. Stroking his chin, the head of the Merchants Guild smiled and leaned towards Mr. Lin.

"There's something I've been wanting to talk to you about for a long time, but I never had the opportunity. I don't know where Guomindang Commissioner Bu saw your daughter, but he's very interested in her. Commissioner Bu is forty and he had no sons. Though he has two women at home, neither of them has been able to give birth. If your daughter should join his household and present him with a child, he's sure to make her his wife, Madam Commissioner. Ah, if that should happen, even I could share in the reflected glory!"

Never in his wildest dreams had Mr. Lin ever imagined he would run into trouble like this. He was speechless. The head of the Merchants Guild continued solemnly:

"We're old friends. There's nothing we can't speak freely about to each other. This kind of thing, according to the old standards, would make you lose face. But it isn't altogether like that any more; it's quite common nowadays. Your daughter's going over could be considered proper marriage. Anyhow, since that is what Commissioner Bu has in

位不懂什麼的，倒也難以對付；一個是老頭子，兩個是孤苦的女人，軟說不肯，硬來又不成。林先生想了半天覺得只有去找商會長，請他去和那三位寶貝講開。他和壽生說了，壽生也竭力贊成。

於是晚飯後算過了當天的「流水賬」，林先生就去拜訪商會長。

林先生說明了來意後，那商會長一口就應承了，還誇獎林先生做生意的手段高明，他那鋪子一定能夠站住，而且上進。摸着自己的下巴，商會長又笑了一笑，偏過身體來說道：

「有一件事，早就想對你說，只是沒有機會。鎮上的卜局長不知在哪裏見過令嬡來，極為中意；卜局長年將四十，還沒有兒子，屋子裏雖則放着兩個人，都沒生育過；要是令嬡過去，生下一男半女，就是現成的局長太太。呵，那時，就連我也沾點兒光呢！」

林先生做夢也想不到會有這樣的難題，當下怔住了做不得聲。商會長卻又鄭重地接着說：

「我們是老朋友。什麼話都可以講個明白。論到這種事呢，照老派說，好像面子上不好聽；然而也不盡然。現在通行這一套，令嬡過去也算是正的。——況且，卜局長既然有了這個心，不答應他有

mind, there might be some inconvenience if you refuse him. If you agree, you can have real hope for the future. I wouldn't be telling you this if I didn't have your interests at heart."

"Of course in advising me to be careful, your intentions are the best! But I'm an unimportant person, my daughter knows nothing of high society. We don't dare aspire so high as a commissioner!" Mr. Lin had to brace himself up to speak. His heart was thumping fast.

"Ha ha! It isn't a question of your aspirations, but the fact that he finds her suitable.... Let's leave it at that. You go home and talk it over with your wife. I'll put the matter aside. When I see Commissioner Bu I'll say I haven't had a chance to speak to you about it, alright? But you must give me an answer soon!"

There was a long pause. Then, "I will," Mr. Lin forced himself to say. His face was ghastly.

When he got home, he sent his daughter out of the room and reported to his wife in detail. Even before he finished, Mrs. Lin's hiccups rose in a powerful barrage that was probably audible to all the neighbours. With an effort she stemmed the tide and said, panting:

"How can we consent? — hic — Even if it wasn't concubine he wanted — hic — hic — even if he were looking for a wife, I still couldn't bear to part with her!"

"That's the way I feel, but — "

"Hic — we run our business all legal and proper. Do you mean to say if we don't agree he could get away with taking her by force? Hic — "

"But he's sure to find an excuse to make some kind of trouble. That kind of man is crueler than a bandit!" Mr. Lin whispered. He was nearly crying.

許多不便之處；答應了，將來倒有巴望。我是替你打算，才說這個話。」

「咳，你怕不是好意勸我仔細！可是，我是小戶人家，小女又不懂規矩，高攀卜局長，實在不敢！」

林先生硬着頭皮說，心裏卜卜亂跳。

「哈，哈，不是你高攀，是他中意。——就這麼罷，你回去和尊夫人商量商量，我這裏且擱着，看見卜局長時，就說還沒機會提過，行不行呢？可是你得早點給我回音！」

「嗯——」

籌思了半晌，林先生勉強應着，臉色像是死人。

回到家裏，林先生支開了女兒，就一五一十對林大娘說了。他還沒說完，林大娘的呃就大發作，光景鄰舍都聽得清。她勉強抑住了那些湧上來的呃，喘着氣說道：

「怎麼能夠答應，呃，就不是小老婆，呃，呃——我也捨不得阿秀到人家去做媳婦。」

「我也是這個意思，不過——」

「呃，我們規規矩矩做生意，呃，難道我們不肯，他好搶了去不成？呃——」

「不過他一定要來找訛頭生事！這種人比強盜還狠心！」

林先生低聲說，幾乎落下眼淚來。

"He'll get her only over my dead body! Hic! Goddess Guanyin preserve us!" cried Mrs. Lin in a voice that trembled. She rose and started to sway out of the room. Mr. Lin hastily barred her way.

"Where are you going? Where are you going?" he babbled.

Just then, Miss Lin came in. Obviously she had overheard quite a bit, for her complexion was the colour of chalk and her eyes were staring fixedly. Mrs. Lin flung her arms around her daughter and wept and hiccuped while she struggled to say in gasps:

"Hic — child — hic — anybody who tries to snatch you — hic — will have to do it over my dead body! Hic! The year I gave birth to you I got this — sickness — hic — It was hard, but I brought you up till now you're seventeen — hic — hic — Dead or alive, we'll stick together! Hic! We should have promised you to Shousheng long ago! Hic! That Bu is a dirty crook! He isn't afraid the gods will strike him down!"

Miss Lin wept too, crying "Ma!" Mr. Lin wrung his hands and sighed. The women were wailing at an alarming rate, and he was afraid their laments would be heard through the thin walls and startle the neighbours. This sort of row was also an unlucky way to commence the new year. Holding his own emotions in check, he did his best to soothe wife and daughter.

That night, all three members of the Lin family slept badly. Although Mr. Lin had to get up early the next morning to go to business, he wrestled with his gloomy thoughts all night. A sudden sound on the roof sent his heart leaping with fear that Commissioner Bu had come to trump up charges against him. Then he calmed himself and considered the matter carefully. His was a family of proper business people who had never committed any crimes. As long as he did a good business and didn't owe people money, surely Bu couldn't make trouble without any reason at all. And now Lin's business was

「我拚了這條老命。呃！救苦救難觀世音呀！」

林大娘顫着聲音站了起來，搖搖擺擺想走。林先生趕快攔住，沒口地叫道：「往哪裏去？往哪裏去？」

同時林小姐也從房外來了，顯然已經聽見了一些，臉色灰白，眼睛死瞪瞪地。林大娘看見女兒，就一把抱住了，一邊哭，一邊打呃，一邊喃喃地掙扎着喘着氣説：

「呃，阿囡，呃，誰來搶你去，呃，我同他拚老命！呃，生你那年我得了這個——病，呃，好容易養到十七歲，呃，呃，死也死在一塊兒！呃，早給了壽生多麼好呢！呃！強盜！不怕天打的！」

林小姐也哭了，叫着「媽！」林先生搓着手嘆氣。看看哭得不像樣，窄房淺屋的要驚動鄰舍，大新年也不吉利，他只好忍着一肚子氣來勸母女兩個。

這一夜，林家三口兒都沒有好生睡覺。明天一早林先生還得起來做生意，在一夜的轉側愁思中，他偶爾聽得屋面上一聲響，心就卜卜地跳，以為是卜局長來尋他生事來了；然而定了神仔細想起來，自家是規規矩矩的生意人，又沒犯法，只要生意好，不欠人家的錢，難道好無端生事，白詐他不成？而他的生意呢，眼前分明有

beginning to show some vitality. Just because he had raised a good-looking daughter, he had invited disaster! He should have engaged her years ago, then maybe this problem would never have arisen.... Was the head of the Merchants Guild sincerely willing to help? The only way out was to beg for his aid — Mrs. Lin started hiccuping again. Ai! That ailment of hers!

Mr. Lin rose as soon as the sky began to turn light. His eyes were somewhat bloodshot and swollen, and he felt dizzy. But he had to pull himself together and attend to business. He couldn't leave the entire management of the shop to Shousheng; the young fellow had put in an exhausting few days.

He was still uneasy after he seated himself in the cashier's cage. Although business was good, from time to time his whole body was shaken by violent shivers. Whenever a big man came in, if Mr. Lin didn't know him, he would suspect that the man had been sent by Commissioner Bu to spy, to stir up a fuss, and his heart would thump painfully.

And it was strange. Business that day was active beyond all expectations. By noon they had sold nearly sixty dollars' worth of merchandise. There were local townspeople among the customers too. They weren't just buying; they were practically grabbing. The only thing like it would be a bankrupt shop selling its stock out at auction cheap. While Mr. Lin was fairly pleased, he was also rather alarmed. This kind of business didn't look healthy to him. Sure enough, Shousheng approached him during the lunch hour and said softly:

"There's a rumour outside that you've cut prices to clear out your left-overs. That when you've collected a little money, you're going to take it and run!"

Mr. Lin was both angry and frightened. He couldn't speak. Suddenly two men in uniform entered and barged forward to demand:

一線生機。生了個女兒長的還端正，卻又要招禍！早些定了親，也許不會出這岔子？──商會長是不是肯真心幫忙呢，只有懇求他設法──可是林大娘又在打呃了，咳，她這病！

天剛發白，林先生就起身，眼圈兒有點紅腫，頭裏發昏。可是他不能不打起精神招呼生意。鋪面上靠壽生一個到底不行，這小伙子近幾天來也就累得夠了。

林先生坐在賬台裏，心總不定。生意雖然好，他卻時時渾身的肉發抖。看見面生的大漢子上來買東西，他就疑惑是卜局長派來的人，來偵察他，來尋事；他的心直跳得發痛。

卻也作怪，這天生意之好，出人意料。到正午，已經賣了五六十元，買客們中間也有本鎮人。那簡直不像買東西，簡直是搶東西，只有倒閉了鋪子拍賣底貨的時候才有這種光景。林先生一邊有點高興，一邊卻也看着心驚，他估量「這樣的好生意氣色不正」。果然在午飯的時候，壽生就悄悄告訴道：

「外邊又有謠言，說是你拆爛污賣一批賤貨，撈到幾個錢，就打算逃走！」

林先生又氣又怕，開不得口。突然來了兩個穿制服的人，直闖進來問道：

"Which one is Mr. Lin, the proprietor?"

Mr. Lin rose in flurred haste. Before he had a chance to reply, the uniformed men began to lead him away. Shousheng came over to stop them and to question them. They barked at him savagely:

"Who are you? Stand aside! He's wanted for questioning at the Guomindang office!"

VI

That afternoon, Mr. Lin did not return. They were busy at the shop, and Shousheng could not get away to inquire personally. He had managed to conceal the truth from Mrs. Lin but one of the apprentices let it leak out, and the lady became frantic almost to the point of distraction. She absolutely refused to let Miss Lin go out of the swinging doors.

"They've already taken your father. They'll be coming back for you next! Hic — "

She called in Shousheng and questioned him closely. He didn't think it advisable to tell her too much.

"Don't worry, Mrs. Lin," he comforted. "There's nothing wrong! He only went down to the Guomindang office to straighten out the question of our creditors. Business is good. What have we got to be afraid of!"

Behind Mrs. Lin's back, he told Miss Lin quietly, "We still don't

「誰是林老闆？」

林先生慌忙站了起來，還沒回答，兩個穿制服的拉住他就走。壽生追上去，想要攔阻，又想要探詢，那兩個人厲聲吆喝道：

「你是誰？滾開！黨部裏要他問話！」

那天下午，林先生就沒回來。店裏生意忙，壽生又不能抽空身子盡自去探聽。裏邊林大娘本來還被瞞着，不防小學徒漏了嘴，林大娘那一急幾乎一口氣死去。她又死不放林小姐出那對蝴蝶門兒，說是：

「你的爸爸已經被他們捉去了，回頭就要來搶你！呃——」

她只叫壽生進來問底細，壽生瞧着情形不便直說，只含糊安慰了幾句道：

「師母，不要着急，沒有事的！師傅到黨部裏去理直那些存款呢。我們的生意好，怕什麼的！」

背轉了林大娘的面，壽生悄悄告訴林小姐，「到底為什麼，還沒

really know what this is all about." He urged her to look after her mother; he would attend to the shop. Miss Lin didn't have the faintest idea what to do. She agreed to everything Shousheng said.

Between waiting on the customers and thinking up answers to Mrs. Lin's constant questions, it was impossible for Shousheng to find time to inquire about the fate of Mr. Lin. Finally, at twilight, word was brought by the head of the Merchants Guild: Mr. Lin was being held by the Guomindang chieftains because of the rumour that he was planning to abscond with the shop's money. Besides what Mr. Lin owed the bank and the wholesale house, there were also his three poor creditors to be considered. The total of six hundred and fifty dollars which they had put up was in jeopardy. The Guomindang was especially concerned over the welfare of these poor people. So it was detaining him until he settled with them.

Shousheng's face was drained of colour. Dazed, he finally managed to ask:

"Can we put up a guarantee and have him released first? Unless we get him out, how are we going to raise the money?"

"Huh! Release him on a guarantee! You can't become his guarantor if you go there without money in your hands!"

"Mr. Guild Leader, think of something, I beg you. Do a good deed. You and Mr. Lin are old friends. I beg you to help him!"

The head of the Merchants Guild frowned thoughtfully. He looked at Shousheng for a minute, then led him to a corner of the room and said in a low voice:

"I can't stand by with folded arms and watch Mr. Lin remain in difficulty. But the situation is very strained now! To tell you the truth, I've already pleaded with Commissioner Bu to intervene.

得個準信兒，」他叮囑林小姐且安心伴着「師母」，外邊事有他呢。林小姐一點主意也沒有，壽生說一句，她就點一下頭。

這樣又要招顧外面的生意，又要挖空心思找出話來對付林大娘不時的追詢，壽生更沒有工夫去探聽林先生的下落。直到上燈時分，這才由商會長給他一個信：林先生是被黨部扣住了，為的外邊謠言林先生打算捲款逃走，然而林先生除有莊款和客賬未清外，還有朱三阿太、橋頭陳老七、張寡婦三位孤苦人兒的存款共計六百五十元沒有保障，黨部裏是專替這些孤苦人兒謀利益的，所以把林先生扣起來，要他理直這些存款。

壽生嚇得臉都黃了，呆了半晌，方才問道：

「先把人保出來，行麼？人不出來，哪裏去弄錢來呢？」

「嘿！保出人來！你空手去，讓你保麼？」

「會長先生，總求你想想法子，做好事。師傅和你老人家向來交情也不差，總求你做做好事！」

商會長皺着眉頭沉吟了一會兒，又端相着壽生半晌，然後一把拉壽生到屋角裏悄悄說道：

「你師傅的事，我豈有袖手旁觀之理。只是這件事現在弄僵了！老實對你說，我求過卜局長出面講情，卜局長只要你師傅答應一件

Commissioner Bu only wanted Mr. Lin to agree to one thing, and would be willing to help him. I've just seen Mr. Lin at the Guomindang office where I urged him to consent, and he did so. Shouldn't that be the end of the matter? Who would have thought that dark pock-marked fellow in the Guomindang would be so nasty? He still insists — "

"Surely he wouldn't go against Commissioner Bu?"

"That's what I thought! But the pock-marked fellow kept mumbling and grumbling till Commissioner Bu was very embarrassed. They had a terrible row! Now you see how awkward things are?"

Shousheng sighed. He had no idea. There was a pause, then he sighed again and said:

"But Mr. Lin hasn't committed any crime."

"Those people don't talk reason! With them, might makes right! Tell Mrs. Lin not to worry; Mr. Lin hasn't been mistreated yet. But to get him out she'll have to spend a little money!"

The head of the Merchants Guild held up two fingers, then quickly departed.

Though he racked his brains, Shousheng could see no other alternative. The two salesmen plagued him with questions, but he ignored them. He was wondering whether he should report the words of the head of the Merchants Guild to Mrs. Lin. Again they had to spend money! While he didn't know quite clear as to the financial condition of the shop: After the local bank got through deducting its eighty per cent from the cash earned during the past two days, all that was left for the shop was about fifty dollars. A lot of good that would do! The head of the Merchants Guild had indicated a bribe of two hundred dollars. Who knew whether that would be enough! The way things were, even if business should improve even more, it still

事，他是肯幫忙的；我剛才到黨部裏會見你的師傅，勸他答應，他也答應了，那不是事情完了麼？不料黨部裏那個黑麻子真可惡，他硬不肯——」

「難道他不給卜局長面子？」

「就是呀！黑麻子反而嚕哩嚕囌說了許多，卜局長幾乎下不得台。兩個人鬧翻了！這不是這件事弄得僵透？」

壽生嘆了口氣，沒有主意；停一會兒，他又嘆一口氣說：

「可是師傅並沒犯什麼罪。」

「他們不同你講理！誰有勢，誰就有理！你去對林大娘說，放心，還沒吃苦，不過要想出來，總得花點兒錢！」

商會長說着，伸兩個指頭一揚，就匆匆地走了。

壽生沉吟着，沒有主意；兩個夥計攢住他探問，他也不回答。商會長這番話，可以告訴「師母」麼？又得花錢！「師母」有沒有私蓄，他不知道；至於店裏，他很明白，兩天來賣得的現錢，被恆源提了八成去，剩下只有五十多塊，濟得什麼事！商會長示意總得兩

wouldn't be any use. Shousheng felt discouraged.

From the back room, someone was calling him. He decided to go in and size up the situation, and then determined what should be done. He found Mrs. Lin leaning on her daughter's arm.

"Hic — just now — hic — the head of the Merchants Guild came — hic — " she panted. "What did he say?"

"He wasn't here," lied Shousheng.

"You can't fool me — hic — I — hic — know everything. Hic — your face is scared yellow! Xiu saw him — hic!"

"Be calm, Mrs. Lin. He says it's all right. Commissioner Bu is willing to help — "

"What? Hic — hic — What? Commissioner Bu is willing to help! — Hic, hic — Merciful goddess — hic — I don't want his help! Hic, hic — I know — Mr. Lin — hic, hic — is finished! Hic — I want to die too! There's only Xiu — hic — that I'm worried about! Hic, hic — take her with you! — Hic! You two go and get married! Hic — hic — Shousheng — hic — you take good care of Xiu and I won't worry about anything! Hic! Go! They want to grab her! — Hic — the savage beasts! Goddess Guanyin, why don't you display your divine power!"

Shousheng stared. He didn't know what to say. He thought Mrs. Lin had gone mad, yet she didn't look the least abnormal. His heart beating hard, he stole a glance at Miss Lin. She was blushing scarlet; she kept her head down and made no comment.

"Shousheng, Shousheng, somebody wants to see you!" an apprentice came running in and announced.

Thinking it was the head of the Merchants Guild or some such personage, Shousheng rushed out. To his surprise, he found Mr. Wu,

百。知道還夠不夠呀！照這樣下去，生意再好些也不中用。他覺得有點灰心了。

裏邊又在叫他了！他只好進去瞧光景再定主意。

林大娘扶住了女兒的肩頭，氣喘喘地問道：

「呃，剛才，呃——商會長來了，呃，説什麼？」

「沒有來呀！」

壽生撒一個謊。

「你不用瞞我，呃——我，呃，全知道了；啊，你的臉色嚇得焦黃！阿秀看見的，呃！」

「師母放心，商會長説過不要緊。——卜局長肯幫忙——」

「什麼？呃，呃——什麼？卜局長肯幫忙！——呃，呃，大慈大悲的菩薩，呃，不要他幫忙！呃，呃，我知道，你的師傅，呃呃，沒有命了！呃，我也不要活了！呃，只是這阿秀，呃，我放心不下！呃，呃，你同了她去！呃，你們好好的做人家！呃，呃，壽生，呃，你待阿秀好，我就放心了！呃，去呀！他們要來搶！呃——狠心的強盜！觀世音菩薩怎麼不顯靈呀！」

壽生睜大了眼睛，不知道怎樣回話。他以為「師母」瘋了，但可又一點不像瘋。他偷眼看他的「師妹」，心裏有點跳；林小姐滿臉通紅，低了頭不作聲。

「壽生哥，壽生哥，有人找你説話！」

小學徒一路跳着喊進來。壽生慌忙跑出去，總以為又是商會長什麼的來了，哪裏知道竟是斜對門裕昌祥的掌櫃吳先生。「他來幹什

proprietor of the shop across the street, waiting for him. What does he want? wondered Shousheng. He fixed his eyes on Mr. Wu's face.

Mr. Wu inquired about Mr. Lin, and then, all smiles, said he was sure it was "not serious." Shousheng felt there was something fishy about his smile.

"I've come to buy a little of your merchandise — " The smile had disappeared from Mr. Wu's face and the tone of his voice changed. He produced a sheet of paper from his sleeve. It was a list of over a dozen items — the very things Mr. Lin was featuring in his "One Dollar Package." One look and Shousheng understood. So that was the game!

"Mr. Lin isn't here," he said promptly. "I haven't the right to decide."

"Why not talk to Mrs. Lin? That'll be just as good!"

Shousheng hesitated to reply. He was beginning to have an inkling of why Mr. Lin had been detained. First there was the rumour that Mr. Lin was planning to run away, then Mr. Lin was arrested, and now the competitor's shop had come to gouge merchandise. There was an obvious connection between these events. Shousheng became rather angry, and a bit frightened. He knew that if he agreed to Mr. Wu's request, Mr. Lin's business would be finished, and the heart's blood that he himself had expended would be in vain. But if he refused, what other tricks would be forthcoming? He simply didn't dare to think.

"I'll go and talk to Mrs. Lin, then," he offered tentatively. "But she only operates on a cash basis."

"Cash? Ha, Shousheng, of course you're joking?"

"That's the kind of person Mrs. Lin is. I can't do anything with her. The best thing would be for you to come again tomorrow. The

麼？」壽生肚子裏想，眼光盯住在吳先生的臉上。

吳先生問過了林先生的消息，就滿臉笑容，連說「不要緊」。壽生覺得那笑臉有點異樣。

「我是來找你劃一點貨——」

吳先生收了笑容，忽然轉了口氣，從袖子裏摸出一張紙來。是一張橫單，寫着十幾行，正是林先生所賣「一元貨」的全部。壽生一眼瞧見就明白了，原來是這個把戲呀！他立刻說：

「師傅不在，我不能作主。」

「你和你師母說，還不是一樣！」壽生躊躇着不能回答。他現在有點懂得林先生之所以被捕了。先是謠言林先生要想逃，其次是林先生被扣住了，而現在卻是裕昌祥來挖貨，這一連串的線索都明白了。壽生想來有點氣，又有點怕，他很知道，要是答應了吳先生的要求，那麼，林先生的生意，自己的一番心血，都完了。可是不答應呢，還有什麼把戲來，他簡直不敢想下去了。最後他姑且試一試說：

「那麼，我去和師母說，可是，師母女人家專要做現錢交易。」

「現錢麼？哈，壽生，你是說笑話罷？」

「師母是這種脾氣，我也是沒法。最好等明天再談罷。剛才商會

head of the Merchants Guild just told me that Commissioner Bu is willing to take a hand in the matter. Mr. Lin probably will be back tonight," said Shousheng with cold deliberateness. He shoved the list back in Mr. Wu's hand.

His face twitching, the latter hastily forced the list on Shousheng again.

"All right, all right, if it has to be cash then it's cash. I'll take the goods tonight. Cash on delivery."

Scowling, Shousheng walked into the back room and told Mrs. Lin about the shop across the street wanting to gouge merchandise.

"When the head of the Merchants Guild was here, he really said Mr. Lin was fine; he hasn't been through any hardships. But we'll have to spend some money to get him out. There's only fifty dollars in the shop. Now this fellow across the street wants goods — from the looks of his list, about a hundred and fifty dollars' worth. Why not let him have them? The important thing is to get Mr. Lin back as soon as possible! "

Upon hearing that they had to spend money again, tears gushed from Mrs. Lin's eyes, and her hiccups truly shook the heavens with their intensity. Beyond words, she could only wave her hand, while her head, which she rested on the table, resounded alarmingly against the wooden top. Shousheng could see that he was getting nowhere, and he quietly withdrew. Miss Lin caught up with him outside the swinging doors. Her face was deathly white, her voice trembling and hoarse.

"Ma is so angry she can't think straight," Miss Lin whispered urgently. "She keeps saying they're already killed Papa! You, you hurry up and agree to what Mr. Wu wants. Save Papa, quick! Shousheng, Brother, you — " At this point, her face suddenly flamed scarlet, and she flew back into the room.

長説，卜局長肯幫忙講情，光景師傅今晚上就可以回來了。」

壽生故意冷冷的説，就把那張橫單塞還吳先生的手裏。吳先生臉上的肉一跳，慌忙把橫單又推回到壽生手裏，一面沒口應承道：

「好，好，現賬就是現賬。今晚上交貨，就是現賬。」壽生皺着眉頭再到裏邊，把裕昌祥來挖貨的事情對林大娘説了，並且勸她：

「師母，剛才商會長來，確實説師傅好好的在那裏，並沒吃苦；不過總得花幾個錢，才能出來。店裏只有五十塊。現在裕昌祥來挖貨，照這單子上看，總也有一百五十塊光景，還是挖給他們罷，早點救師傅出來要緊！」

林大娘聽説又要花錢，眼淚直淌，那一陣呃，當真打得震天響，她只是搖手，説不出話，頭靠在桌子上，把桌子搥得怪響。壽生瞧來不是路，悄悄的退出去，但在蝴蝶門邊，林小姐追上來了。她的臉色像死人一樣白，她的聲音抖而且啞，她急口地説：

「媽是氣糊塗了！總説爸爸已經被他們弄死了！你，你趕快答應裕昌祥，趕快救爸爸！壽生哥，你──」

林小姐説到這裏，忽然臉一紅，就飛快地跑進去了。壽生望着

In a daze, Shousheng stared after her for a full half minute, then he turned away, determined to take the responsibility for selling the merchandise to their competitor. At least Miss Lin agreed with him on what should be done.

The table had already been laid for dinner in the shop, but Shousheng had no appetite. As soon as Mr. Wu arrived with the money, Shousheng took one hundred dollars in his hand and concealed another eighty dollars on his person, and rushed off to find the head of the Merchants Guild.

Half an hour later Shousheng returned with Mr. Lin. Bursting into the "inner sanctum," they nearly startled Mrs. Lin out of her wits. When she saw that it was really Mr. Lin in the flesh, she agitatedly prostrated herself before the porcelain Guanyin and kowtowed vigorously, pounding her head so loudly that it drowned out the sound of her hiccups. Miss Lin stood to one side, her eyes staring. She looked as if she wanted to laugh and cry at the same time. Shousheng took out a paper-wrapped packet and set it on the table.

"This is eighty dollars we didn't have to use."

Mr. Lin sighed. When he finally spoke, his voice was dull.

"You should have let me die there and be done with it. Spending more money to get me out! Now we've got no money, we're all going to die anyhow! "

Mrs. Lin jumped up from the ground, excited and wanting to speak. But a string of hiccups blocked the words in her throat. Miss Lin wept quietly, with suppressed sobs. Mr. Lin did not cry. He sighed again and said in a choked voice:

"Our merchandise has been cleaned out! We can't do any business, they're pressing us hard for debts — "

她的後影，呆立了半分鐘光景，然後轉身，下決心擔負這挖貨給裕昌祥的責任，至少「師妹」是和他一條心要這麼辦了。

夜飯已經擺在店鋪裏了，壽生也沒有心思吃，立等着裕昌祥交過錢來，他拿一百在手裏，另外身邊藏了八十，就飛跑去找商會長。

半點鐘後，壽生和林先生一同回來了。跑進「內宅」的時候，林大娘看見了倒嚇一跳。認明是當真活的林先生時，林大娘急急爬在瓷觀音前磕響頭，比她打呃的聲音還要響。林小姐光着眼睛站在旁邊，像是要哭，又像是要笑。壽生從身旁掏出一個紙包來，放在桌子上說：

「這是多下來的八十塊錢。」

林先生嘆了一口氣，過一會兒，方才有聲沒氣地說道：

「讓我死在那邊就是了，又花錢弄出來！沒有錢，大家還是死路一條！」

林大娘突然從地下跳起來，着急的想說話，可是一連串的呃把她的話塞住了。林小姐忍住了聲音，抽抽咽咽地哭。林先生卻還不哭，又嘆一口氣，哽咽着說：

「貨是挖空了！店開不成，債又逼的緊──」

"Mr. Lin!"

It was Shousheng who shouted. He dipped his finger in the tea, then wrote on the table the one word — "Go."

Mr. Lin shook his head. Tears flowed from his eyes. He looked at his wife, he looked at his daughter, and again he sighed.

"That's the only way out, Mr. Lin! We can still scrape together a hundred dollars in the shop. Take it with you; it'll be enough for a month or two. I'll take care of what has to be done here."

Although Shousheng spoke quietly, Mrs. Lin overheard him. She curbed her hiccups and interjected:

"You go too, Shousheng! You and Xiu. Leave me here alone. I'll fight to the death! Hic!"

Mrs. Lin suddenly appeared remarkably young and healthy; she whirled and ran up the stairs. "Ma!" called Miss Lin, and dashed after her mother. Mr. Lin stared at the stairway, bewildered. He felt he had something important to say, but he was too numb to recall what it was.

"You and Xiu go together," Shousheng urged softly.

"Mrs. Lin will worry if Xiu stays here! She says they want to snatch — "

Tears in his eyes, Mr. Lin nodded. He couldn't make up his mind.

Shousheng felt his own eyes smarting. He sighed and walked around the table.

Just then, they heard Miss Lin crying. Startled, Mr. Lin and Shousheng rushed up the stairs. Mrs. Lin was coming out of her room with a paper packet in her hand. She went back into the room when she saw them, and said:

「師傅！」

壽生叫了一聲，用手指蘸着茶，在桌子上寫了一個「走」字給林先生看。

林先生搖頭，眼淚撲簌簌地直淌；他看看林大娘，又看看林小姐，又嘆一口氣。

「師傅！只有這一條路了。店裏拼湊起來，還有一百塊，你帶了去，過一兩個月也就夠了；這裏的事，我和他們理直。」

壽生低聲說。可是林大娘卻偏偏聽得了，她忽然抑住了呃，搶着叫道：

「你們也去！你，阿秀。放我一個人在這裏好了，我拚老命！呃！」

忽然異常少健起來，林大娘轉身跑到樓上去了。林小姐叫着「媽」，隨後也追了上去。林先生望着樓梯發怔，心裏感到有什麼要緊的事，卻又亂麻麻地總是想不起。壽生又低聲說：

「師傅，你和師妹一同走罷！師妹在這裏，師母是不放心的！她總說他們要來搶——」

林先生淌着眼淚點頭，可是打不起主意。

壽生忍不住眼圈兒也紅了，嘆一口氣，繞着桌子走。

忽然聽得林小姐的哭聲。林先生和壽生都一跳。他們趕到樓梯頭時，林大娘卻正從房裏出來，手裏捧一個皮紙包兒。看見林先生和壽生都已在樓梯頭了，她就縮回房去，嘴裏說「你們也來，聽我的主意」。她當着林先生和壽生的跟前，指着那紙包說道：

"Please come in, both of you. Listen to what I've decided." She pointed at the packet. "In here is my private property — hic — about two hundred dollars. I'm giving you two half. Hic! Xiu, I give you in marriage to Shousheng! Hic — tomorrow, Xiu and her father will leave together. Hic — I'm not going! Shousheng will stay with me a few days, and then we'll see. Who knows how many days I have left to live — hic — So if you both kowtow in my presence, I can set my mind at ease! Hic — "

Mrs. Lin took her daughter by one hand and Shousheng by the other, and ordered them to "kowtow." Both did so, their cheeks flaming red; they kept their heads down. Shousheng stole a glance at Miss Lin. There was a faint smile on her tear-stained face. His heart thumped wildly, and two tears rolled down from his eyes.

"Good. That's the way it'll be." Mr. Lin heaved a sigh. "But Shousheng, when you stay here and deal with those people, be very, very careful!"

VII

The shop of the Lin family had to close down at last. The news that Mr. Lin had run away soon spread all over town. Of the creditors, the local bank was the first to send people to put the stock into custody. They also searched for the account books. Not one was to be found. They asked for Shousheng. He was sick in bed. They grilled Mrs. Lin. Her reply was a string of explosive hiccups and a stream of tears. Since she after all enjoyed the social position of "Madam Lin," there was nothing they could do with her.

「這是我的私房，呃，光景有兩百多塊。分一半你們拿去。呃！阿秀，我做主配給壽生！呃，明天阿秀和她爸爸同走。呃，我不走！壽生陪我幾天再説。呃，知道我還有幾天活，呃，你們就在我面前拜一拜，我也放心！呃——」

林大娘一手拉着林小姐，一手拉着壽生，就要他們「拜一拜」。

都拜了，兩個人臉上飛紅，都低着頭。壽生偷眼看林小姐，看見她的淚痕中含着一些笑意，壽生心頭卜卜地跳了，反倒落下兩滴眼淚。

林先生鬆一口氣，説道；

「好罷，就是這樣。可是壽生，你留在這裏對付他們，萬事要細心！」

七

林家鋪子終於倒閉了。林老闆逃走的新聞傳遍了全鎮。債權人中間的恆源莊首先派人到林家鋪子裏封存底貨。他們又搜尋賬簿。一本也沒有了。問壽生。壽生躺在牀上害病。又去逼問林大娘。林大娘的回答是連珠炮似的打呃和眼淚鼻涕。為的她到底是「林大娘」，人們也沒有辦法。

By about eleven a.m., the horde of creditors in the Lin shop were quarrelling with a tremendous din. The local bank and the other creditors were wrangling as to how to divide the remaining property. Although the stock was nearly gone, the remainder and the furniture and fixture were enough to repay the creditors about seventy per cent; but each was fighting for a ninety, or even one hundred, per cent for himself. The head of the Merchants Guild had talked until his tongue was a little paralysed, to no avail.

Two policemen arrived and took their stand outside the shop door. Clubs in hand, they barked at the crowed that had gathered to see the excitement.

"Why can't I go in? I've got a three hundred dollar loan in this shop! My savings!" Mrs. Zhu argued with a policeman, twisting her withered lips. Tottering, she was elbowing her way through the mass. The blue veins on her forehead stood out as thick as little fingers. She kept pushing. Then suddenly she saw Widow Zhang, with her five-year-old baby in her arms, pleading with the other policeman to let her enter. He looked at the widow out of the corners of his eyes, and while feigning to tease the child, furtively rubbed the back of his hand against the widow's breasts.

"Sister Zhang — " Mrs. Zhu gasped loudly. She sat down on the edge of the stone steps, forcibly moving her puckered mouth.

Tears in her eyes, Widow Zhang took an aimless step, which brought into her line of vision Mrs. Zhu panting on the edge of the stone stairs. She practically stumbled over to Mrs. Zhu and sat down beside her. Then, Widow Zhang began to cry and lament:

"Oh, my husband, you've left me alone! You don't know how I'm suffering! The wicked soldiers killed you — it was three years ago the day before yesterday…. That cursed Mr. Lin — may he die without

十一點鐘光景，大群的債權人在林家鋪子裏吵鬧得異常厲害。恆源莊和其他的債權人爭執怎樣分配底貨。鋪子裏雖然淘空，但連「生財」合計，也足夠償還債權者七成，然而誰都只想給自己爭得九成或竟至十成。商會長說得舌頭都有點僵硬了，卻沒有結果。

來了兩個警察，拿着木棍站在門口吆喝那些看熱鬧的閒人。

「怎麼不讓我進去？我有三百塊錢的存款呀！我的老本！」

朱三阿太扭着癟嘴唇和警察爭論，巍顫顫地在人堆裏擠。她額上的青筋就有小指頭兒那麼粗。她擠了一會兒，忽然看見張寡婦抱着五歲的孩子在那裏哀求另一個警察放她進去。那警察斜着眼睛，假裝是調弄那孩子，卻偷偷地用手背在張寡婦的乳部揉摸。

「張家嫂呀——」

朱三阿太氣喘喘地叫了一聲，就坐在石階沿上，用力地扭着她的癟嘴唇。

張寡婦轉過身來，找尋是誰喚她；那警察卻用了褻昵的口吻叫道：

「不要性急！再過一會兒就進去！」

聽得這句話的閒人都笑起來了。張寡婦裝作不懂，含着一泡眼淚，無目的地又走了一步。恰好看見朱三阿太坐在石階沿上喘氣。張寡婦跌撞似的也到了朱三阿太的旁邊，也坐在那石階沿上，忽然就放聲大哭。她一邊哭，一邊喃喃地訴說着：

「阿大的爺呀，你丟下我去了，你知道我是多麼苦啊！強盜兵打殺了你，前天是三周年……絕子絕孫的林老闆又倒了鋪子，——我

sons or grandsons! — has closed his shop! The hundred and fifty dollars that I earned by the toil of my two hands has fallen into the sea and is gone without a sound! Aiya! The lot of the poor is hard, and the rich have no hearts — "

Hearing his mother cry, the child also began to wail. Widow Zhang hugged him to her bosom and wept even more bitterly.

Mrs. Zhu did not cry. Her sunken red-rimmed eyes glared, and she kept saying frantically:

"The poor have only one life, and the rich have only one life. If they don't give me back my money, I'll fight them to the death! "

Just then, a man pushed his way out of the shop. It was Old Chen. His face was purple. He was cursing as he jostled through the crowd.

"You gang of crooks! You'll pay for this! One day I'll see you all burning in the fires of Hell! If we have to take a loss, everybody should take it together. Even if I got only a small share of what's left, at least that would be fair — "

Still swearing vigorously, he spotted the two women.

"Mrs. Zhang, Mrs. Zhu, what are you sitting there crying for!" he shouted to them. "They've finished dividing up the property. My one mouth couldn't out-argue their dozen. That pack of jackals doesn't give a damn about what's reasonable. They insist that our money doesn't count — "

His words made Widow Zhang weep more bitterly than ever. The playful policeman abruptly walked over to her. He poked her shoulder with his club.

"Hey, what are you crying about? Your man died a long time ago. Which one are you crying for now!"

十個指頭做出來的百幾十塊錢，丟在水裏了，也沒響一聲！啊喲！窮人命苦，有錢人心狠——」

看見媽哭，孩子也哭了；張寡婦摟住了孩子，哭的更傷心。

朱三阿太卻不哭，弩起了一對發紅的已經凹陷的眼睛，發瘋似的反覆說着一句話：

「窮人是一條命，有錢人也是一條命；少了我的錢，我拚老命！」

此時有一個人從鋪子裏擠出來，正是橋頭陳老七。他滿臉紫青，一邊擠，一邊回過頭去嚷罵道：

「你們這伙強盜！看你們有好報！天火燒，地火爆，總有一天現在我陳老七眼睛裏呀！要吃倒賬，就大家吃，分攤到一個邊皮兒，也是公平，——」

陳老七正罵得起勁，一眼看見了朱三阿太和張寡婦，就叫着她們的名字說：

「三阿太，張家嫂，你們怎麼坐在這裏哭！貨色，他們分完了！我一張嘴吵不過他們十幾張嘴，這班狗強盜不講理，硬說我們的錢不算賬，——」

張寡婦聽說，哭得更加苦了。先前那個警察忽然又踅過來，用木棍子撥着張寡婦的肩膀說：

「喂，哭什麼？你的養家人早就死了。現在還哭哪一個！」

"Dog farts!" roared Old Chen furiously. "While those people are stealing our money, all a turd like you can do is get gay with women! " He gave the policeman a strong push.

The policeman's nasty eyes went wide. He raised his club to strike, but the crowd yelled and cursed at him. The other policeman ran over and pulled Old Chen to one side.

"It's no use your raising a fuss. We've got nothing against you. The Merchants Guild has ordered us to guard the door. We've got to eat. We can't help it."

"Old Chen, go make a complaint at the Guomindang office!" a man shouted from the crowd. From the sound of it, it was the voice of Lu, the well-known loafer.

"Go on, go on!" yelled several others. "See what they say to that!"

The policeman who had mediated laughed coldly. He grasped Old Chen by the shoulder. "I advise you not to go looking for trouble. Going there won't do you any good! You wait till Mr. Lin comes back and settle things with him. He can't deny the debt."

Old Chen fumed. He couldn't make up his mind. The idlers were still shouting for him to "go." He looked at Mrs. Zhu and Widow Zhang.

"What do you say? They're always screaming down there how they protect the poor!"

"That's right," called one of the crowd. "Yesterday they arrested Mr. Lin because they said they didn't want him to run away with poor people's money!"

Almost involuntarily, Old Chen and the two women were swept along by the crowed down the street to the Guomindang office. Widow

「狗屁！人家搶了我們的，你這東西也要來調戲女人麼？」

陳老七怒沖沖地叫起來，用力將那警察推了一把。那警察睜圓了怪眼睛，揚起棍子就想要打。閒人們都大喊，罵那警察。另一個警察趕快跑來，拉開了陳老七說：

「你在這裏吵，也是白吵。我們和你無怨無仇，商會裏叫來守門，吃這碗飯，沒辦法。」

「陳老七，你到黨部裏去告狀罷！」

人堆裏有一個聲音這麼喊。聽聲音就知道是本街有名的閒漢陸和尚。

「去，去！看他們怎樣說。」

許多聲音亂叫了。但是那位作調人的警察卻冷笑，扳着陳老七的肩膀道：

「我勸你少找點麻煩罷。到那邊，中什麼用！你還是等候林老闆回來和他算賬，他倒不好白賴。」

陳老七虎起了臉孔，弄得沒有主意了。經不住那些閒人們都攛慂着「去」，他就看着朱三阿太和張寡婦說道：

「去去怎樣？那邊是天天大叫保護窮人的呀！」

「不錯。昨天他們扣住了林老闆，也是說防他逃走，窮人的錢沒有着落！」

又一個主張去的拉長了聲音叫。於是不由自主似的，陳老七他們三個和一群閒人都向黨部所在那條路去了。張寡婦一路上還是啼

Zhang was crying as she walked, and cursing the wicked soldiers who had killed her husband, and praying that Mr. Lin should die without sons or grandsons, and reviling that dirty dog of a policeman!

As they neared the office, they saw four policemen standing outside the gate with clubs in their hands. The policemen yelled to them from a distance:

"Go home! You can't go in!"

"We've come to make a complaint!" shouted Old Chen, who was in the first rank of the crowd. "The shop of the Lin family has closed down, and we can't get hold of the money we put to — "

A swarthy pock-marked man jumped out from behind the policemen and howled for them to attack. But the policemen stood their ground, restricting themselves to threats. The crowd in back of Old Chen began to clamour.

"You cheap mongrels don't know what's good for you!" screamed the pock-marked man. "Do you think we have nothing better to do than bother about your business? If you don't get out of here, we're going to fire!"

He stamped and yelled at the policemen to use their clubs. In the front ranks, Old Chen was struck several times. The crowd milled in confusion. Mrs. Zhu was old and weak, and she toppled to the ground. In her panicky haste, Widow Zhang lost her slippers. Pushed and buffeted, she also fell down. Rolling and crawling, she avoided many leaping and stamping feet. She scrambled up and ran for all she was worth. It was then she realized that her child was gone. There were drops of blood on the upper part of her jacket.

"Aiya! My precious! My heart! The bandits are killing people! Jade Emperor God save us!"

哭，咒罵打殺了她丈夫的強盜兵，咒罵絕子絕孫的林老闆，又咒罵那個惡狗似的警察。

快到了目的地時，望見那門前排立着四個警察，都拿着棍子，遠遠地就吆喝道：

「滾開！不准過來！」

「我們是來告狀的，林家鋪子倒了，我們存在那裏的錢都拿不到——」

陳老七走在最前排，也高聲的説。可是從警察背後突然跳出一個黑麻子來，怒聲喝打。警察們卻還站着，只用嘴威嚇。陳老七背後的鬧人們大噪起來。黑麻子怒叫道：

「不識好歹的賤狗！我們這裏管你們那些事麼？再不走，就開槍了！」

他跺着腳喝那四個警察動手打。陳老七是站在最前，已經挨了幾棍子。鬧人們大亂。朱三阿太老邁，跌倒了。張寡婦慌忙中落掉了鞋子，給人們一衝，也跌在地下，她連滾帶爬躲過了許多跳過的和踏上來的腳，站起來跑了一段路，方才覺到她的孩子沒有了。看衣襟上時，有幾滴血。

「啊喲！我的寶貝！我的心肝！強盜殺人了，玉皇大帝救命呀！」

Wailing, her hair tumbled in disorder, she ran quickly. By the time she fled past the closed door of the shop of the Lin family, she was completely out of her mind.

June 18, 1932

她帶哭帶嚷的快跑，頭髮紛散；待到她跑過那倒閉了的林家鋪面時，她已經完全瘋了！

1932年6月18日作完

春 蠶

Spring Silkworms

Spring Silkworms

Old Tong Bao sat on a rock beside the road that skirted the canal, his long-stemmed pipe lying on the ground next to him. Though it was only a few days after "Clear and Bright Festival" the April sun was already very strong. It scorched Old Tong Bao's spine like a basin of fire. Straining down the road, the men towing the fast junk wore only thin tunics, open in front. They were bent far forward, pulling, pulling, pulling, great beads of sweat dripping from their brows.

The sight of others toiling strenuously made Old Tong Bao feel even warmer; he began to itch. He was still wearing the tattered padded jacket in which he had passed the winter. His unlined jacket had not yet been redeemed from the pawn shop. Who would have believed it could get so hot right after "Clear and Bright"?

Even the weather's not what it used to be, Old Tong Bao said to himself, and spat emphatically.

Before him, the water of the canal was green and shiny. Occasional passing boats broke the mirror-smooth surface into ripples and eddies, turning the reflection of the earthen bank and the long line of mulberry trees flanking it into a dancing grey blur. But not for long! Gradually the trees reappeared, twisting and weaving drunkenly. Another few minutes, and they were again standing still, reflected as clearly as

春　蠶

　　老通寶坐在「塘路」邊的一塊石頭上，長旱煙管斜擺在他身邊。「清明」節後的太陽已經很有力量，老通寶背脊上熱烘烘地，像背着一盆火。「塘路」上拉縴的快班船上的紹興人只穿了一件藍布單衫，敞開了大襟，彎着身子拉，額角上黃豆大的汗粒落到地下。

　　看着人家那樣辛苦的勞動，老通寶覺得身上更加熱了；熱的有點兒發癢。他還穿着那件過冬的破棉襖，他的夾襖還在當鋪裏，卻不防才得「清明」邊，天就那麼熱。

　　「真是天也變了！」

　　老通寶心裏說，就吐一口濃厚的唾沫。在他面前那條「官河」內，水是綠油油的，來往的船也不多，鏡子一樣的水面這裏那裏起了幾道皺紋或是小小的渦旋，那時候，倒影在水裏的泥岸和岸邊成排的桑樹，都攪亂成灰暗的一片。可是不會很長久的。漸漸兒那些樹影又在水面上顯現，一彎一曲地蠕動，像是醉漢，再過一會兒，

before. On the gnarled fists of the mulberry branches, little fingers of tender green buds were already bursting forth. Crowded close together, the trees along the canal seemed to march endlessly into the distance. The unplanted fields as yet were only cracked colds of dry earth; the mulberry trees reigned supreme here this time of the year! Behind Old Tong Bao's back was another great stretch of mulberry trees, squat, silent. The little buds seemed to be growing bigger every second in the hot sunlight.

Not far from where Old Tong Bao was sitting, a grey twostorey building crouched beside the road. That was the silk filature, where the delicate fibres were removed from the cocoons. Two weeks ago it was occupied by troops; a few short trenches still scarred the fields around it. Everyone had said that the Japanese soldiers were attacking in this direction. The rich people in the market town had all run away. Now the troops were gone and the silk filature stood empty and locked as before. There would be no noise and excitement in it again until cocoon selling time.

Old Tong Bao had heard Young Master Chen — son of the Master Chen who lived in town — say that Shanghai was seething with unrest, that all the silk weaving factories had closed their doors, that the silk filatures here probably wouldn't open either. But he couldn't believe it. He had been through many periods of turmoil and strife in his sixty years, yet he had never seen a time when the shiny green mulberry leaves had been allowed to wither on the branches and become fodder for the sheep. Of course if the silkworm eggs shouldn't ripen, that would be different. Such matters were all in the hands of the Old Lord of the Sky. Who could foretell His will?

"Only just after Clear and Bright and so hot already!" marvelled Old Tong Bao, gazing at the small green mulberry leaves. He was happy as well as surprised. He could remember only one year when it was

終於站定了，依然是很清晰的倒影。那拳頭模樣的椏枝頂都已經簇生着小手指兒那麼大的嫩綠葉。這密密層層的桑樹，沿着那「官河」一直望去，好像沒有盡頭。田裏現在還只有乾裂的泥塊，這一帶，現在是桑樹的勢力！在老通寶背後，也是大片的桑林，矮矮的，靜穆的，在熱烘烘的太陽光下，似乎那「桑拳」上的嫩綠葉過一秒鐘就會大一些。

離老通寶坐處不遠，一所灰白色的樓房蹲在「塘路」邊，那是繭廠。十多天前駐紮過軍隊，現在那邊田裏留着幾條短短的戰壕。那時都説東洋兵要打進來，鎮上有錢人都逃光了；現在兵隊又開走了，那座繭廠依舊空關在那裏，等候春繭上市的時候再熱鬧一番。老通寶也聽得鎮上小陳老爺的兒子——陳大少爺説過，今年上海不太平，絲廠都關門，恐怕這裏的繭廠也不能開；但老通寶是不肯相信的。他活了六十歲，反亂年頭也經過好幾個，從沒見過綠油油的桑葉白養在樹上等到成了「枯葉」去餵羊吃；除非是「蠶花」不熟，但那是老天爺的「權柄」，誰又能夠未卜先知？

「才得清明邊，天就那麼熱！」

老通寶看着那些桑拳上怒苗的小綠葉兒，心裏又這麼想，同時有幾分驚異，有幾分快活。他記得自己還是二十多歲少壯的時候，

too hot for padded clothes at Clear and Bright. He was in his twenties then, and the silkworn eggs had hatched "two hundred per cent"! That was the year he got married. His family was flourishing in those days. His father was like an experienced plough ox — there was nothing he didn't understand, nothing he wasn't willing to try. Even his old grandfather — the one who had first started the family on the road to prosperity — seemed to be growing more hearty with age, in spite of the hard time he was said to have had during the years he was a prisoner of the "Long Hairs."

Old Master Chen was still alive then. His son, the present Master Chen, hadn't begun smoking opium yet, and the "House of Chen" hadn't become the bad lot it was today. Moreover, even though the House of Chen was of the rich gentry and his own family only ordinary tillers of the land, Old Tong Bao had felt that the destinies of the two families were linked together. Years ago, "Long Hairs" campaigning through the countryside had captured Tong Bao's grandfather and Old Master Chen and kept them working as prisoners for nearly seven years in the same camp. They had escaped together, taking a lot of the "Long Hairs'" gold with them — people still talk about it to this day. What's more, at the same time Old Master Chen's silk trade began to prosper, the cocoon raising of Tong Bao's family grew successful too. Within ten years grandfather had earned enough to buy three acres of rice paddy, two acres of mulberry grove, and build a modest house. Tong Bao's family was the envy of the people of East Village, just as the House of Chen ranked among the first families in the market town.

But afterwards, both families had declined. Today, Old Tong Bao had no land of his own, in fact he was over three hundred silver dollars in debt. The House of Chen was finished too. People said the spirit of the dead "Long Hairs" had sued the Chens in the underworld, and because the King of Hell had decreed that the Chens repay the fortune

有一年也是「清明」邊就得穿夾，後來就是「蠶花二十四分」，自己也
就在這一年成了家。那時，他家正在「發」；他的父親像一頭老牛似
的，什麼都懂得，什麼都做得；便是他那創家立業的祖父，雖說在
長毛窩裏吃過苦頭，卻也愈老愈硬朗。那時候，老陳老爺去世不
久，小陳老爺還沒抽上鴉片煙，「陳老爺家」也不是現在那麼不像樣
的。老通寶相信自己一家和「陳老爺家」雖則一邊是高門大戶，而一
邊不過是種田人，然而兩家的命運好像是一條線兒牽着。不但「長毛
造反」那時候，老通寶的祖父和陳老爺同被長毛擄去，同在長毛窩裏
混上了六七年，不但他們倆同時從長毛營盤裏逃了出來，而且偷得
了長毛的許多金元寶——人家到現在還是這麼說；並且老陳老爺做
絲生意「發」起來的時候，老通寶家養蠶也是年年都好，十年中間掙
得了二十畝的稻田和十多畝的桑地，還有三開間兩進的一座平屋。
這時候，老通寶家在東村莊上被人人所妒羨，也正像「陳老爺家」在
鎮上是數一數二的大戶人家。可是以後，兩家都不行了；老通寶現
在已經沒有自己的田地，反欠出三百多塊錢的債，「陳老爺家」也早
已完結。人家都說「長毛鬼」在陰間告了一狀，閻羅王追還「陳老爺

they had amassed on the stolen gold, the family had gone down financially very quickly. Old Tong Bao was rather inclined to believe this. If it hadn't been for the influence of devils, why would a decent fellow like Master Chen have taken to smoking opium?

What Old Tong Bao could never understand was why the fall of the House of Chen should affect his own family. They certainly hadn't kept any of the "Long Hairs'" gold. True, his father had related that when grandfather was escaping from the "Long Hairs'" camp he had run into a young "Long Hair" on patrol and had to kill him. What else could he have done? It was "fate"! Still from Tong Bao's earliest recollections, his family had prayed and offered sacrifices to appease the soul of the departed young "Long Hair" time and time again. That little wronged spirit should have left the nether world and been reborn long ago by now! Although Old Tong Bao couldn't recall what sort of man his grandfather was, he knew his father had been hardworking and honest — he had seen that with his own eyes. Old Tong Bao himself was a respectable person; both A Si, his elder son, and his daughter-in-law were industrious and frugal. Only his younger son, A Duo, was inclined to be a little flighty. But youngsters were all like that. There was nothing really bad about the boy....

Old Tong Bao raised his wrinkled face, scorched by years of hot sun to the colour of dark parchment. He gazed bitterly at the canal before him, at the boats on its waters, at the mulberry trees along its banks. All were approximately the same as they had been when he was twenty. But the world had changed. His family now often had to make their meals of pumpkin instead of rice. He was over three hundred silver dollars in debt....

Toot! Toot-toot-toot....

Far up the bend in the canal a boat whistle broke the silence. There was a silk filature over there too. He could see vaguely the neat lines

家」的金元寶橫財，所以敗的這麼快。這個，老通寶也有幾分相信：不是鬼使神差，好端端的小陳老爺怎麼會抽上了鴉片煙？

可是老通寶死也想不明白為什麼「陳老爺家」的「敗」會牽動到他家。他確實知道自己家並沒得過長毛的橫財。雖則聽死了的老頭子說，好像那老祖父逃出長毛營盤的時候，不巧撞着了一個巡路的小長毛，當時沒法，只好殺了他，──這是一個「結」！然而從老通寶懂事以來，他們家替這小長毛鬼拜忏唸佛燒紙錠，記不清有多少了。這個小冤魂，理應早投凡胎。老通寶雖然不很記得祖父是怎樣「做人」，但父親的勤儉忠厚，他是親眼看見的；他自己也是規矩人，他的兒子阿四，兒媳四大娘，都是勤儉的。就是小兒子阿多年紀青，有幾分「不知苦辣」，可是毛頭小伙子，大都這麼着，算不得「敗家相」！

老通寶抬起他那焦黃的皺臉，苦惱地望着他面前的那條河，河裏的船，以及兩岸的桑地。一切都和他二十多歲時差不了多少，然而「世界」到底變了。他自己家也要常常把雜糧當飯吃一天，而且又欠出了三百多塊錢的債。

嗚！嗚，嗚，嗚，──

汽笛叫聲突然從那邊遠遠的河身的彎曲地方傳了來。就在那邊，蹲着又一個繭廠，遠望去隱約可見那整齊的石「幫岸」。一條柴

of stones embedded as reinforcement in the canal bank. A small oil-burning river boat came puffing up pompously from beyond the silk filature, tugging three larger craft in its wake. Immediately the peaceful water was agitated with waves rolling towards the banks on both sides of the canal. A peasant, poling a tiny boat, hastened to shore and clutched a clump of reeds growing in the shallows. The waves tossed him and his little craft up and down like a see-saw. The peaceful green countryside was filled with the chugging of the boat engine and the stink of its exhaust.

Hatred burned in Old Tong Bao's eyes. He watched the river boat approach, he watched it sail past and glared after it until it went tooting around another bend and disappeared from sight. He had always abominated the foreign devils' contraptions. He himself had never met a foreign devil, but his father had given him a description of one Old Master Chen had seen — red eyebrows, green eyes and a stiff-legged walk! Old Master Chen had hated the foreign devils too. "The foreign devils have swindled our money away," he used to say. Old Tong Bao was only eight or nine the last time he saw Old Master Chen. All he remembered about him now were things he had heard from others. But whenever Old Tong Bao thought of that remark — "The foreign devils have swindled our money away" — he could almost picture Old Master Chen, stroking his beard and wagging his head.

How the foreign devils had accomplished this, Old Tong Bao wasn't too clear. He was sure, however, that Old Master Chen was right. Some things he himself had seen quite plainly. From the time foreign goods — cambric, cloth, oil — appeared in the market town, from the time the foreign river boats increased on the canal, what he produced brought a lower price in the market every day, while what he had to buy became more and more expensive. That was why the property his father left him had shrunk until it finally vanished completely;

油引擎的小輪船很威嚴地從那繭廠後駛出來，拖着三條大船，迎面向老通寶來了。滿河平靜的水立刻激起潑刺刺的波浪，一齊向兩旁的泥岸捲過來。一條鄉下「赤膊船」趕快攏岸，船上人揪住了泥岸上的樹根，船和人都好像在那裏打秋千。軋軋軋的輪機聲和洋油臭，飛散在這和平的綠的田野。老通寶滿臉恨意，看着這小輪船來，看着它過去，直到又轉一個彎，嗚嗚嗚地又叫了幾聲，就看不見。老通寶向來仇恨小輪船這一類洋鬼子的東西！他從沒見過洋鬼子，可是他從他的父親嘴裏知道老陳老爺見過洋鬼子：紅眉毛，綠眼睛，走路時兩條腿是直的。並且老陳老爺也是很恨洋鬼子，常常説「銅鈿都被洋鬼子騙去了」。老通寶看見老陳老爺的時候，不過八九歲，——現在他所記得的關於老陳老爺的一切都是聽來的，可是他想起了「銅鈿都被洋鬼子騙去了」這句話，就彷彿看見了老陳老爺捋着鬍子搖頭的神氣。

洋鬼子怎樣就騙了錢去，老通寶不很明白。但他很相信老陳老爺的話一定不錯。並且他自己也明明看到自從鎮上有了洋紗，洋布，洋油，——這一類洋貨，而且河裏更有了小火輪船以後，他自己田裏生出來的東西就一天一天不值錢，而鎮上的東西卻一天一天貴起來。他父親留下來的一份家產就這麼變小，變做沒有，而且現

and now he was in debt. It was not without reason that Old Tong Bao hated the foreign devils!

In the village, his attitude towards foreigners was well known. Five years before, in 1927, someone had told him: The new Kuomintang government says it wants to "throw out" the foreign devils. Old Tong Bao didn't believe it. He heard those young propaganda speech makers the Kuomintang sent when he went into the market town. Though they cried "Throw out the foreign devils," they were dressed in Western style clothing. His guess was that they were secretly in league with the foreign devils, that they had been purposely sent to delude the countryfolk! Sure enough, the Kuomintang dropped the slogan not long after, and prices and taxes rose steadily. Old Tong Bao was firmly convinced that all this occurred as part of a government conspiracy with the foreign devils.

Last year something had happened that made him almost sick with fury: Only the cocoons spun by the foreign strain silkworms could be sold at a decent price. Buyers paid ten dollars more per load for them than they did for the local variety. Usually on good terms with his daughter-in-law, Old Tong Bao had quarrelled with her because of this. She had wanted to raise only foreign silkworms, and Old Tong Bao's younger son A Duo had agreed with her. Though A Si didn't say much, in his heart he certainly had also favoured this course. Events had proved they were right, and they wouldn't let Old Tong Bao forget it. This year, he had to compromise. Of the five trays they would raise, only four would be silkworms of the local variety; one tray would contain foreign silkworms. "The world's going from bad to worse! In another couple of years they'll even be wanting foreign mulberry trees! It's enough to take all the joy out of life!"

Old Tong Bao picked up his long pipe and rapped it angrily against a cold of dry earth. The sun was directly overhead now, foreshortening

在負了債。老通寶恨洋鬼子不是沒有理由的！他這堅定的主張，在村坊上很有名。五年前，有人告訴他：朝代又改了，新朝代是要「打倒」洋鬼子的。老通寶不相信。為的他上鎮去看見那新到的喊着「打倒洋鬼子」的年青人們都穿了洋鬼子衣服。他想來這夥年青人一定私通洋鬼子，卻故意來騙鄉下人。後來果然就不喊「打倒洋鬼子」了，而且鎮上的東西更加一天一天貴起來，派到鄉下人身上的捐稅也更加多起來。老通寶深信這都是串通了洋鬼子幹的。

然而更使老通寶去年幾乎氣成病的，是繭子也是洋種的賣得好價錢；洋種的繭子，一擔要貴上十多塊錢。素來和兒媳總還和睦的老通寶，在這件事上可就吵了架。兒媳四大娘去年就要養洋種的蠶。小兒子跟他嫂嫂是一路，那阿四雖然嘴裏不多說，心裏也是要洋種的。老通寶拗不過他們，末了只好讓步。現在他家裏有的五張蠶種，就是土種四張，洋種一張。

「世界真是愈變愈壞！過幾年他們連桑葉都要洋種了！我活得厭了！」

老通寶看着那些桑樹，心裏說，拿起身邊的長旱煙管恨恨地敲

his shadow till it looked like a piece of charcoal. Still in his padded jacket, he was bathed in heat. He unfastened the jacket and swung its opened edges back and forth a few times to fan himself. Then he stood up and started for home.

Behind the row of mulberry trees were paddy fields. Most of them were as yet only neatly ploughed furrows of upturned earth clods, dried and cracked by the hot sun. Here and there, the early crops were coming up. In one field, the golden blossoms of rape-seed plants emitted a heady fragrance. And that group of houses way over there, that was the village where three generations of Old Tong Bao's family were living. Above the houses, white smoke from many kitchen stoves was curling lazily upwards into the sky.

After crossing through the mulberry grove, Old Tong Bao walked along the raised path between the paddy fields, then turned and looked again at that row of trees bursting with tender green buds. A twelve-year-old boy came bounding along from the other end of the fields, calling as he ran:

"Grandpa! Ma's waiting for you to come home and eat!"

It was Little Bao, Old Tong Bao's grandson.

"Coming!" the old man responded, still gazing at the mulberries. Only twice in his life had he seen these finger-like buds appear on the branches so soon after Clear and Bright. His family would probably have a fine crop of silkworms this year. Five trays of eggs would hatch out a huge number of silkworms. If only they didn't have another bad market like last year, perhaps they could pay off part of their debt.

Little Bao stood beside his grandfather. The child too looked at the soft green on the gnarled fist branches. Jumping happily, he clapped his hands and chanted:

着腳邊的泥塊。太陽現在正當他頭頂，他的影子落在泥地上，短短地像一段烏焦木頭，還穿着破棉襖的他，覺得渾身躁熱起來了。他解開了大襟上的鈕扣，又抓着衣角扇了幾下，站起來回家去。

那一片桑樹背後就是稻田。現在大部分是勻整的半翻着的燥裂的泥塊。偶爾也有種了雜糧的，那黃金一般的菜花散出強烈的香味。那邊遠遠地一簇房屋，就是老通寶他們住了三代的村坊，現在那些屋上都裊起了白的炊煙。

老通寶從桑林裏走出來，到田塍上，轉身又望那一片爆着嫩綠的桑樹。忽然那邊田裏跳躍着來了一個十來歲的男孩子，遠遠地就喊道：

「阿爹！媽等你吃中飯呢！」

「哦——」

老通寶知道是孫子小寶，隨口應着，還是望着那一片桑林。才只得「清明」邊，桑葉尖兒就抽得那麼小指頭兒似的，他一生就只見過兩次。今年的蠶花，光景是好年成。三張蠶種，該可以採多少繭子呢？只要不像去年，他家的債也許可以拔還一些罷。

小寶已經跑到他阿爹的身邊了，也仰着臉看那綠絨似的桑拳頭；忽然他跳起來拍着手唱道：

> Green, tender leaves at Clear and Bright,
> The girls who tend silkworms
> Clap hands at the sight!

The old man's wrinkled face broke into a smile. He thought it was a good omen for the little boy to respond like this on seeing the first buds of the year. He rubbed his hand affectionately over the child's shaven pate. In Old Tong Bao's heart, numbed wooden by a lifetime of poverty and hardship, suddenly hope began to stir again.

II

The weather remained warm. The rays of the sun forced open the tender, finger-like, little buds. They had already grown to the size of a small hand. Around Old Tong Bao's village, the mulberry trees seemed to respond especially well. From a distance they gave the appearance of a low grey picket fence on top of which a long swath of green brocade had been spread. Bit by bit, day by day, hope grew in the hearts of the villagers. The unspoken mobilization order for the silkworm campaign reached everywhere and everyone. Silkworm rearing equipment that had been laid away for a year was again brought out to be scrubbed and mended. Beside the little stream which ran through the village, women and children, with much laughter and calling back and forth, washed the implements.

None of these women or children looked really healthy. Since the coming of spring, they had been eating only half their fill; their clothes were old and torn. As a matter of fact, they weren't much better off

「清明削口，看蠶娘娘拍手！」

老通寶的皺臉上露出笑容來了。他覺得這是一個好兆頭。他把手放在小寶的「和尚頭」上摩着，他的被窮苦弄麻木了的老心裏勃然又生出新的希望來了。

天氣繼續暖和，太陽光催開了那些桑拳頭上的小手指兒模樣的嫩葉，現在都有小小的手掌那麼大了。老通寶他們那村莊四周圍的桑林似乎發長得更好，遠望去像一片綠錦平鋪在密密層層灰白色矮矮的籬笆上。「希望」在老通寶和一般農民們的心裏一點一點一天一天強大。蠶事的動員令也在各方面發動了。藏在柴房裏一年之久的養蠶用具都拿出來洗刷修補。那條穿村而過的小溪旁邊，蠕動着村裏的女人和孩子，工作着，嚷着，笑着。

這些女人和孩子們都不是十分健康的臉色，——從今年開春起，他們都只吃個半飽；他們身上穿的，也只是些破舊的衣服。實

than beggars. Yet all were in quite good spirits, sustained by enormous patience and grand illusions. Burdened though they were by daily mounting debts, they had only one thought in their heads — If we get a good crop of silkworms, everything will be all right! ... They could already visualize how, in a month, the shiny green leaves would be converted into snow-white cocoons, the cocoons exchanged for clinking silver dollars. Although their stomachs were growling with hunger, they couldn't refrain from smiling at this happy prospect.

Old Tong Bao's daughter-in-law was among the women by the stream. With the help of her twelve-year-old son, Little Bao, she had already finished washing the family's large trays of woven bamboo strips. Seated on a stone beside the stream, she wiped her perspiring face with the edge of her tunic. A twenty-year-old girl, working with other women on the opposite side of the stream, hailed her:

"Are you raising foreign silkworms this year too?"

It was Sixth Treasure, sister of young Fuqing, the neighbour who lived across the stream.

The thick eyebrows of Old Tong Bao's daughter-in-law at once contracted. Her voice sounded as if she had just been waiting for a chance to let off steam.

"Don't ask me; what the old man says, goes!" she shouted. "He's dead set against it, won't let us raise more than one batch of foreign breed! The old fool only has to hear the word 'foreign' to send him up in the air! He'll take dollars made of foreign silver, though; those are the only 'foreign' things he likes!"

The women on the other side of the stream laughed. From the threshing ground behind them a strapping young man approached.

在他們的情形比叫化子好不了多少。然而他們的精神都很不差。他們有很大的忍耐力，又有很大的幻想。雖然他們都負了天天在增大的債，可是他們那簡單的頭腦老是這麼想：只要蠶花熟，就好了！他們想像到一個月以後那些綠油油的桑葉就會變成雪白的繭子，於是又變成叮叮噹噹響的洋錢，他們雖然肚子裏餓得咕咕地叫，卻也忍不住要笑。

這些女人中間也就有老通寶的媳婦四大娘和那個十二歲的小寶。這娘兒兩個已經洗好了那些「團扁」和「蠶簞」，坐在小溪邊的石頭上撩起布衫角揩臉上的汗水。

「四阿嫂！你們今年也看(養)洋種麼？」

小溪對岸的一群女人中間有一個二十歲左右的姑娘隔溪喊過來了。四大娘認得是隔溪的對門鄰舍陸福慶的妹子六寶。四大娘立刻把她的濃眉毛一挺，好像正想找人吵架似的嚷了起來：

「不要來問我！阿爹做主呢！——小寶的阿爹死不肯，只看了一張洋種！老糊塗的聽得帶一個洋字就好像見了七世冤家！洋錢，也是洋，他倒又要了！」

小溪旁那些女人們聽得笑起來了。這時候有一個壯健的小伙子

He reached the stream and crossed over on the four logs that served as a bridge. Seeing him, his sister-in-law dropped her tirade and called in a high voice:

"A Duo, will you help me carry these trays? They're as heavy as dead dogs when they're wet!"

Without a word, A Duo lifted the six big trays and set them, dripping, on his head. Balancing them in place, he walked off, swinging his hands in a swimming motion. When in a good mood, A Duo refused nobody. If any of the village women asked him to carry something heavy or fish something out of the stream, he was usually quite willing. But today he probably was a little grumpy, and so he walked empty-handed with only six trays on his head. The sight of him, looking as if he were wearing six layers of wide straw hats, his waist twisting at each step in imitation of the ladies of the town, sent the women into peals of laughter. Lotus, wife of Old Tong Bao's nearest neighbour, called with a giggle:

"Hey, A Duo, come back here. Carry a few trays for me too!"

A Duo grinned. "Not unless you call me a sweet name!" He continued walking. An instant later he had reached the porch of his house and set down the trays out of the sun.

"Will 'kid brother' do?" demanded Lotus, laughing boisterously. She had a remarkably clean white complexion, but her face was very flat. When she laughed, all that could be seen was a big open mouth and two tiny slits of eyes. Originally a slavey in a house in town, she had been married off to Old Tong Bao's neighbour — a prematurely aged man who walked around with a sour expression and never said a word all day. That was less than six months ago, but her love affairs and escapades already were the talk of the village.

正從對岸的陸家稻場上走過，跑到溪邊，跨上了那橫在溪面用四根木頭並排做成的雛形的「橋」。四大娘一眼看見，就丟開了「洋種」問題，高聲喊道：

「多多弟！來幫我搬東西罷！這些扁，浸濕了，就像死狗一樣重！」

小伙子阿多也不開口，走過來拿起五六隻「團扁」，濕漉漉地頂在頭上，卻空着一雙手，划槳似的蕩着，就走了。這個阿多高興起來時，什麼事都肯做，碰到同村的女人們叫他幫忙拿什麼重傢伙，或是下溪去撈什麼，他都肯；可是今天他大概有點不高興，所以只頂了五六隻「團扁」去，卻空着一雙手。那些女人們看着他戴了那特別大箬帽似的一疊「扁」，裊着腰，學鎮上女人的樣子走着，又都笑起來了。老通寶家緊鄰的李根生的老婆荷花一邊笑，一邊叫道：

「喂，多多頭！回來！也替我帶一點兒去！」

「叫我一聲好聽的，我就給你拿。」

阿多也笑着回答，仍然走。轉眼間就到了他家的廊下，就把頭上的「團扁」放在廊簷口。

「那麼，叫你一聲乾兒子！」

荷花說着就大聲的笑起來，她那出眾地白淨然而扁得作怪的臉上看去就好像只有一張大嘴和眯緊了好像兩條線一般的細眼睛。她原是鎮上人家的婢女，嫁給那不聲不響整天苦着臉的半老頭子李根生還不滿半年，可是她的愛和男子們胡調已經在村中很有名。

"Shameless hussy!" came a contemptuous female voice from across the stream.

Lotus' piggy eyes immediately widened. "Who said that?" she demanded angrily. "If you've got the brass to call me names, let's see you try it to my face! Come out into the open!"

"Think you can handle me? I'm talking about a shameless, man-crazy baggage! If the shoe fits, wear it!" retorted Sixth Treasure, for it was she who had spoken. She too was famous in the village, but as a mischievous, lively young woman.

The two began splashing water at each other from opposite banks of the stream. Girls who enjoyed a row took sides and joined the battle, while the children whooped with laughter. Old Tong Bao's daughter-in-law was more decorous. She picked up her remaining trays, called to Little Bao and returned home. A Duo watched from the porch, grinning. He knew why Sixth Treasure and Lotus were quarrelling. It did his heart good to hear that sharp-tongued Sixth Treasure get told off in public.

Old Tong Bao came out of the house with a wooden tray-stand on his shoulder. Some of the legs of the uprights had been eaten by termites, and he wanted to repair them. At the sight of A Duo standing there laughing at the women, Old Tong Bao's face lengthened. The boy hadn't much sense of propriety, he well knew. What disturbed him particularly was the way A Duo and Lotus were always talking and laughing together. "That bitch is an evil spirit. Fooling with her will bring ruin on our house," he had often warned his younger son.

"A Duo!" he now barked angrily. "Enjoying the scenery? Your brother's in the back mending equipment. Go and give him a hand!" His inflamed eyes bored into A Duo, never leaving the boy until he disappeared into the house.

「不要臉的！」

忽然對岸那群女人中間有人輕聲罵了一句。荷花的那對細眼睛立刻睜大了，怒聲嚷道：

「罵哪一個？有本事，當面罵，不要躲！」

「你管得我？棺材橫頭踢一腳，死人肚裏自得知：我就罵那不要臉的騷貨！」

隔溪立刻回罵過來了，這就是那六寶，又一位村裏有名淘氣的大姑娘。

於是對罵之下，兩邊又潑水。愛鬧的女人也夾在中間幫這邊幫那邊。小孩子們笑着狂呼。四大娘是老成的，提起她的「蠶簞」，喊着小寶，自回家去。阿多站在廊下看着笑。他知道為什麼六寶要跟荷花吵架；他看着那「辣貨」六寶挨罵，倒覺得很高興。

老通寶捐着一架「蠶台」從屋子裏出來。這三稜形傢伙的木梗子有幾條給白螞蟻蛀過了，怕的不牢，須得修補一下。看見阿多站在那裏笑嘻嘻地望着外邊的女人們吵架，老通寶的臉色就板起來了。他這「多多頭」的小兒子不老成，他知道。尤其使他不高興的，是多多也和緊鄰的荷花說說笑笑。「那母狗是白虎星，惹上了她就得敗家」，——老通寶時常這樣警戒他的小兒子。

「阿多！空手看野景麼？阿四在後邊紮『綴頭』，你去幫他！」

老通寶像一匹瘋狗似的咆哮着，火紅的眼睛一直盯住了阿多的身體，直到阿多走進屋裏去，看不見了，老通寶方才提過那「蠶台」

Only then did Old Tong Bao start work on the tray-stand. After examining it carefully, he slowly began his repairs. Years ago, Old Tong Bao had worked for a time as a carpenter. But he was old now; his fingers had lost their strength. A few minutes' work and he was breathing hard. He raised his head and looked into the house. Five squares of cloth to which sticky silkworm eggs were adhered, hung from a horizontal bamboo pole.

His daughter-in-law, A Si's wife, was at the other end of the porch, pasting paper on big trays of woven bamboo strips. Last year, to economize a bit, they had bought and used old newspaper. Old Tong Bao still maintained that was why the eggs had hatched poorly — it was unlucky to use paper with writing on it for such a prosaic purpose. Writing meant scholarship, and scholarship had to be respected. This year the whole family had skipped a meal and with the money saved, purchased special "tray pasting paper." A Si's wife pasted the tough, gosling-yellow sheets smooth and flat; on every tray she also affixed three little coloured paper pictures, bought at the same time. One was the "Platter of Plenty" ; the other two showed a militant figure on horseback, pennant in hand. He, according to local belief, was the "Guardian of Silkworm Hatching."

"I was only able to buy twenty loads of mulberry leaves with that thirty silver dollars I borrowed on your father's guarantee," Old Tong Bao said to his daughter-in-law. He was still panting from his exertions with the tray-stand. "Our rice will be finished by the day after tomorrow. What are we going to do?"

Thanks to her father's influence with his boss and his willingness to guarantee repayment of the loan, Old Tong Bao was able to borrow the money at a low rate of interest — only twenty-five per cent a month! Both the principal and interest had to be repaid by the end of the silkworm season.

來反覆審察，慢慢地動手修補。木匠生活，老通寶早年是會的；但近來他老了，手指頭沒有勁，他修了一會兒，抬起頭來喘氣，又望望屋裏掛在竹竿上的五張蠶種。

四大娘就在廊簷口糊「蠶簞」。去年他們為的想省幾百文錢，是買了舊報紙來糊的。老通寶直到現在還說是因為用了報紙——不惜字紙，所以去年他們的蠶花不好。今年是特地全家少吃一餐飯，省下錢來買了「糊簞紙」來了。四大娘把那鵝黃色堅韌的紙兒糊得很平貼，然後又照品字式糊上三張小小的花紙——那是跟「糊簞紙」一塊兒買來的，一張印的花色是「聚寶盆」，另兩張都是手執尖角旗的人兒騎在馬上，據說是「蠶花太子」。

「四大娘！你爸爸做中人借來三十塊錢，就只買了二十擔葉。後天米又吃完了，怎麼辦？」

老通寶氣喘喘地從他的工作裏抬起頭來，望着四大娘。那三十塊錢是二分半的月息。總算有四大娘的父親張財發做中人，那債主也就是張財發的東家「做好事」，這才只要了二分半的月息。條件是蠶事完後本利歸清。

A Si's wife finished pasting a tray and placed it in the sun. "You've spent it all on leaves," she said angrily. "We'll have a lot of leaves left over, just like last year!"

"Full of lucky words, aren't you?" demanded the old man, sarcastically. "I suppose every year'll be like last year? We can't get more than a dozen or so loads of leaves from our own trees. With five sets of grubs to feed, that won't be nearly enough."

"Oh, of course, you're never wrong!" she replied hotly. "All I know is with rice we can eat, without it we'll go hungry!" His stubborn refusal to raise any foreign silkworms last year had left them with only the unsalable local breed. As a result, she was often contrary with him.

The old man's face turned purple with rage. After this, neither would speak to the other.

But hatching time was drawing closer every day. The little village's two dozen families were thrown into a state of great tension, great determination, great struggle. With it all, they were possessed of a great hope, a hope that could almost make them forget their hungry bellies.

Old Tong Bao's family, borrowing a little here, getting a little credit there, somehow managed to get by. Nor did the other families eat any better; there wasn't one with a spare bag of rice! Although they had harvested a good crop the previous year, landlords, creditors, taxes, levies, one after another, had cleaned the peasants out long ago. Now all their hopes were pinned on the spring silkworms. The repayment date of every loan they made was set for the "end of the silkworm season."

With high hopes and considerable fear, like soldiers going into a hand-to-hand battle to the death, they prepared for their spring silkworm campaign!

四大娘把糊好了的「蠶簞」放在太陽底下曬，好像生氣似的説：

「都買了葉！又像去年那樣多下來——」

「什麼話！你倒先來發利市了！年年像去年麼？自家只有十來擔葉；五張布子(蠶種)，十來擔葉夠麼？」

「噢，噢；你總是不錯的！我只曉得有米燒飯，沒米餓肚子！」

四大娘氣哄哄地回答；為了那「洋種」問題，她到現在常要和老通寶抬槓。

老通寶氣得臉都紫了。兩個人就此再沒有一句話。

但是「收蠶」的時期一天一天逼進了。這二三十人家的小村落突然呈現了一種大緊張，大決心，大奮鬥，同時又是大希望。人們似乎連肚子餓都忘記了。老通寶他們家東借一點，西賒一點，居然一天一天過着來。也不僅老通寶他們，村裏哪一家有兩三斗米放在家裏呀！去年秋收固然還好，可是地主、債主、正税、雜捐，一層一層地剝削來，早就完了。現在他們唯一的指望就是春蠶，一切臨時借貸都是指明在這「春蠶收成」中償還。

他們都懷着十分希望又十分恐懼的心情來準備這春蠶的大搏戰！

"Grain Rain" day — bringing gentle drizzles — was not far off. Almost imperceptibly, the silkworm eggs of the two dozen village families began to show faint tinges of green. Women, when they met on the public threshing ground, would speak to one another agitatedly in tones that were anxious yet joyful.

"Over at Sixth Treasure's place, they're almost ready to incubate their eggs!"

"Lotus says her family is going to start incubating tomorrow. So soon!"

"Huang 'the Priest' has made a divination. He predicts that this spring mulberry leaves will go to four dollars a load!"

Old Tong Bao's daughter-in-law examined their five sets of eggs. They looked bad. The tiny seed-like eggs were still pitch black, without even a hint of green. Her husband, A Si, took them into the light to peer at them carefully. Even so, he could find hardly any ripening eggs. She was very worried.

"You incubate them anyhow. Maybe this variety is a little slow," her husband forced himself to say consolingly.

Her lips pressed tight, she made no reply.

Old Tong Bao's wrinkled face sagged with dejection. Though he said nothing, he thought their prospects were dim.

The next day, A Si's wife again examined the eggs. Ha! Quite a few were turning green, and a very shiny green at that! Immediately, she told her husband, told Old Tong Bao, A Duo ... she even told her son Little Bao. Now the incubating process could begin! She held the five pieces of cloth to which the eggs were adhered against her bare bosom. As if cuddling a nursing infant, she sat absolutely quiet, not daring to stir. At night, she took the five sets to bed with her. Her husband was

「穀雨」節一天近一天了。村裏二三十人家的「布子」都隱隱現出綠色來。女人們在稻場上碰見時，都匆忙地帶着焦灼而快樂的口氣互相告訴道：

「六寶家快要『窩種』了呀！」

「荷花說她家明天就要『窩』了。有這麼快！」

「黃道士去測一字，今年的青葉要貴到四洋！」

四大娘看自家的五張「布子」。不對！那黑芝麻似的一片細點子還是黑沉沉，不見綠影。她的丈夫阿四拿到亮處去細看，也找不出幾點「綠」來。四大娘很着急。

「你就先『窩』起來罷！這餘杭種，作興是慢一點的。」

阿四看着他老婆，勉強自家寬慰。四大娘堵起了嘴巴不回答。

老通寶哭喪着乾皺的老臉，沒說什麼，心裏卻覺得不妙。

幸而再過了一天，四大娘再細心看那「布子」時，哈，有幾處轉成綠色了！而且綠的很有光彩。四大娘立刻告訴了丈夫，告訴了老通寶，多多頭，也告訴了她的兒子小寶。她就把那些布子貼肉搵在胸前，抱着吃奶的嬰孩似的靜靜兒坐着，動也不敢多動了。夜間，她抱着那五張布子到被窩裏，把阿四趕去和多多頭做一床。那布子

routed out, and had to share A Duo's bed. The tiny silkworm eggs were very scratchy against her flesh. She felt happy and a little frightened, like the first time she was pregnant and the baby moved inside her. Exactly the same sensation!

Uneasy but eager, the whole family waited for the eggs to hatch. A Duo was the only exception. We're sure to hatch a good crop, he said, but anyone who thinks we're going to get rich in this life, is out of his head. Though the old man swore A Duo's big mouth would ruin their luck, the boy stuck to his guns.

A clean dry shed for the growing grubs was all prepared. The second day of incubation, Old Tong Bao smeared a garlic with earth and placed it at the foot of the wall inside the shed. If, in a few days, the garlic put out many sprouts, it meant the eggs would hatch well. He did this every year, but this year he was more reverential than usual, and his hands trembled. Last year's divination had proved all too accurate. He didn't dare to think about that now.

Every family in the village was busy "incubating." For the time being there were few women's footprints on the threshing ground or the banks of the little stream. An unofficial "martial law" had been imposed. Even peasants normally on very good terms stopped visiting one another. For a guest to come and frighten away the spirits of the ripening eggs — that would be no laughing matter! At most, people exchanged a few words in low tones when they met, then quickly separated. This was the "sacred" season!

Old Tong Bao's family was on pins and needles. In the five sets of eggs a few grubs had begun wriggling. It was exactly one day before Grain Rain. A Si's wife had calculated that most of the eggs wouldn't hatch until after that day. Before or after Grain Rain was all right, but for eggs to hatch on the day itself was considered highly unlucky. Incubation was no longer necessary, and the eggs were carefully placed

上密密麻麻的蠶子兒貼着肉，怪癢癢的；四大娘很快活，又有點兒害怕，她第一次懷孕時胎兒在肚子裏動，她也是那樣半驚半喜的！

全家都是惴惴不安地又很興奮地等候「收蠶」。只有多多頭例外。他説：今年蠶花一定好，可是想發財卻是命裏不曾來。老通寶罵他多嘴，他還是要説。

蠶房早已收拾好了。「窩種」的第二天，老通寶拿一個大蒜頭塗上一些泥，放在蠶房的牆腳邊；這也是年年的慣例，但今番老通寶更加虔誠，手也抖了。去年他們「卜」的非常靈驗。可是去年那「靈驗」，現在老通寶想也不敢想。

現在這村裏家家都在「窩種」了。稻場上和小溪邊頓時少了那些女人們的蹤跡。一個「戒嚴令」也在無形中頒佈了；鄉農們即使平日是最好的，也不往來；人客來衝了蠶神不是玩的！他們至多在稻場上低聲交談一二句就走開。這是個「神聖」的季節。

老通寶家的五張布子上也有些「烏娘」蠕蠕地動了。於是全家的空氣，突然緊張。那正是「穀雨」前一日。四大娘料來可以挨過了「穀雨」節那一天。布子不須再「窩」了，很小心地放在「蠶房」裏。老通寶

in the special shed. Old Tong Bao stole a glance at his garlic at the foot of the wall. His heart dropped. There were still only the same two small green shoots the garlic had originally! He didn't dare to look any closer. He prayed silently that by noon the day after tomorrow the garlic would have many, many more shoots.

At last hatching day arrived. A Si's wife set a pot of rice on to boil and nervously watched for the time when the steam from it would rise straight up. Old Tong Bao lit the incense and candles he had bought in anticipation of this event. Devoutly, he placed them before the idol of the Kitchen God. His two sons went into the fields to pick wild flowers. Little Bao chopped a lamp-wick into fine pieces and crushed the wild flowers the men brought back. Everything was ready. The sun was entering its zenith; steam from the rice pot puffed straight upwards. A Si's wife immediately leaped to her feet, stuck a "sacred" paper flower and a pair of goose feathers into the knot of hair at the back of her head and went to the shed. Old Tong Bao carried a wooden scale-pole; A Si followed with the chopped lamp-wick and the crushed wild flowers. Daughter-in-law uncovered the cloth pieces to which the grubs were adhered, and sprinkled them with the bits of wick and flowers A Si was holding. Then she took the wooden scale-pole from Old Tong Bao and hung the cloth pieces over it. She next removed the pair of goose feathers from her hair. Moving them lightly across the cloth, she brushed the grubs, together with the crushed lamp-wick and wild flowers, on to a large tray. One set, two sets ... the last set contained the foreign breed. The grubs from this cloth were brushed on to a separate tray. Finally, she removed the "sacred" paper flower from her hair and pinned it, with the goose feathers, against the side of the tray.

A solemn ceremony! One that had been handed down through the ages! Like warriors taking an oath before going into battle! Old Tong Bao and family now had ahead of them a month of fierce combat,

偷眼看一下那個躺在牆腳邊的大蒜頭，他心裏就一跳。那大蒜頭上
還只有一兩莖綠芽！老通寶不敢再看，心裏禱祝後天正午會有更多
更多的綠芽。

終於「收蠶」的日子到了。四大娘心神不定地淘米燒飯，時時看
飯鍋上的熱氣有沒有直衝上來。老通寶拿出預先買了來的香燭點起
來，恭恭敬敬放在灶君神位前。阿四和阿多去到田裏採野花。小小
寶幫着把燈芯草剪成細末子，又把採來的野花揉碎。一切都準備齊
全了時，太陽也近午刻了，飯鍋上水蒸氣嘟嘟地直衝，四大娘立刻
跳了起來，把「蠶花」和一對鵝毛插在髮髻上，就到「蠶房」裏。老通
寶拿着秤桿，阿四拿了那揉碎的野花片兒和燈芯草碎末。四大娘揭
開「布分」，就從阿四手裏拿過那野花碎片和燈芯草末子撒在「布子」
上，又接過老通寶手裏的秤桿來，將「布子」挽在秤桿上，於是拔下
髮髻上的鵝毛在布子上輕輕兒拂；野花片，燈芯草末子，連同「烏
娘」，都拂在那「蠶簞」裏了。一張，兩張，……都拂過了；最後一張
是洋種，那就收在另一個「蠶簞」裏。末了，四大娘又拔下髮髻上那
朵「蠶花」，跟鵝毛一塊插在「蠶簞」的邊兒上。

這是一個隆重的儀式！千百年相傳的儀式！那好比是誓師典

with no rest day or night, against bad weather, bad luck and anything else that might come along!

The grubs, wriggling in the trays, looked very healthy. They were all the proper black colour. Old Tong Bao and his daughter-in-law were able to relax a little. But when the old man secretly took another look at his garlic, he turned pale! It had grown only four measly shoots! Ah! Would this year be like last year all over again?

III

But the "fateful" garlic proved to be not so psychic after all. The silkworms of Old Tong Bao's family grew and thrived! Though it rained continuously during the grubs' First Sleep and Second Sleep, and the weather was a bit colder than at Clear and Bright, the "little darlings" were extremely robust.

The silkworms of the other families in the village were not doing badly either. A tense kind of joy pervaded the countryside. Even the small stream seemed to be gurgling with bright laughter. Lotus' family was the sole exception. They were only raising one set of grubs, but by the Third Sleep their silkworms weighed less than twenty catties. Just before the Big Sleep, people saw Lotus' husband walk to the stream and dump out his trays. That dour, old-looking man had bad luck written all over him.

Because of this dreadful event, the village women put Lotus' family strictly "off limits." They made wide detours so as not to pass her door. If they saw her or her taciturn husband, no matter how far away, they made haste to go in the opposite direction. They feared that even

禮，以後就要開始了一個月光景的和惡劣的天氣和惡運以及和不知
什麼的連日連夜無休息的大決戰！

「烏娘」在「蠶簞」裏蠕動，樣子非常強健；那黑色也是很正路
的。四大娘和老通寶他們都放心地鬆一口氣了。但當老通寶悄悄地
把那個「命運」的大蒜頭拿起來看時，他的臉色立刻變了！大蒜頭上
還只得三四莖嫩芽！天哪！難道又同去年一樣？

然而那「命運」的大蒜頭這次竟不靈驗。老通寶家的蠶非常好！
雖然頭眠二眠的時候連天陰雨，氣候是比「清明」邊似乎還要冷一
點，可是那些「寶寶」都很強健。

村裏別人家的「寶寶」也都不差。緊張的快樂瀰漫了全村莊，似
那小溪裏淙淙的流水也像是朗朗的笑聲了。只有荷花家是例外。她
們家看了一張「布子」，可是「出火」只稱得二十斤；「大眠」快邊人們
還看見那不聲不響晦氣色的丈夫根生傾棄了三「蠶簞」在那小溪裏。

這一件事，使得全村的婦人對於荷花家特別「戒嚴」。她們特地
避路，不從荷花的門前走，遠遠的看見了荷花或是她那不聲不響丈

one look at Lotus or her spouse, the briefest conversation, would con-
taminate them with the unfortunate couple's bad luck!

Old Tong Bao strictly forbade A Duo to talk to Lotus. "If I catch
you gabbing with that baggage again, I'll disown you!" he threatened
in a loud, angry voice, standing outside on the porch to make sure
Lotus could hear him.

Little Bao was also warned not to play in front of Lotus' door, and
not to speak to anyone in her family.

The old man harped at A Duo morning, noon and night, but the
boy turned a deaf ear to his father's grumbling. In his heart, he laughed
at it. Of the whole family, A Duo alone didn't place much stock in
taboos and superstitions. He didn't talk with Lotus, however. He was
much too busy for that.

By the Big Sleep, their silkworms weighed three hundred catties.
Every member of Old Tong Bao's family, including twelve-year-old
Little Bao, worked for two days and two nights without sleeping a
wink. The silkworms were unusually sturdy. Only twice in his sixty
years had Old Tong Bao ever seen the like. Once was the year he
married; once when his first son was born.

The first day after the Big Sleep, the "little darlings" ate seven loads
of leaves. They were now a bright green, thick and healthy. Old Tong
Bao and his family, on the contrary, were much thinner, their eyes
bloodshot from lack of sleep.

No one could guess how much the "little darlings" would eat before they spun their cocoons. Old Tong Bao discussed the question of
buying more leaves with A Si.

"Master Chen won't lend us any more. Shall we try your father-in-
law's boss again?"

夫的影兒就趕快躲開；這些幸運的人兒惟恐看了荷花他們一眼或是交談半句話就傳染了晦氣來！

老通寶嚴禁他的小兒子多多頭跟荷花說話。——「你再跟那東西多嘴，我就告你忤逆！」老通寶站在廊簷外高聲大氣喊，故意要叫荷花他們聽得。

小小寶也受到嚴厲的囑咐，不許跑到荷花家的門前，不許和他們說話。

阿多像一個聾子似的不理睬老頭子那早早夜夜的嘮叨，他心裏卻在暗笑。全家就只有他不大相信那些鬼禁忌。可是他也沒有跟荷花說話，他忙都忙不過來。

「大眠」捉了毛三百斤，老通寶全家連十二歲的小寶也在內，都是兩日兩夜沒有合眼。蠶是少見的好，活了六十歲的老通寶記得只有兩次是同樣的，一次就是他成家的那年，又一次是阿四出世那一年。「大眠」以後的「寶寶」第一天就吃了七擔葉，個個是生青滾壯，然而老通寶全家都瘦了一圈，失眠的眼睛上佈滿了紅絲。

誰也料得到這些「寶寶」上山前還得吃多少葉。老通寶和兒子阿四商量了：

「陳大少爺借不出，還是再求財發的東家罷？」

"We've still got ten loads coming. That's enough for one more day," replied A Si. He could barely hold himself erect. His eyelids weighed a thousand catties. They kept wanting to close.

"One more day? You're dreaming!" snapped the old man impatiently. "Not counting tomorrow, they still have to eat three more days. We'll need another thirty loads! Thirty loads, I say!"

Loud voices were heard outside on the threshing ground. A Duo had arrived with men delivering five loads of mulberry branches. Everyone went out to strip the leaves. A Si's wife hurried from the shed. Across the stream, Sixth Treasure and her family were raising only a small crop of silkworms; having spare time, she came over to help. Bright stars filled the sky. There was a slight wind. All up and down the village, gay shouts and laughter rang in the night.

"The price of leaves is rising fast!" a coarse voice cried. "This afternoon, they were getting four dollars a load in the market town!"

Old Tong Bao was very upset. At four dollars a load, thirty loads would come to a hundred and twenty dollars. Where could he raise so much money! But then he figured — he was sure to gather over five hundred catties of cocoons. Even at fifty dollars a hundred, they'd sell for two hundred and fifty dollars. Feeling a bit consoled, he heard a small voice from among the leaf-strippers.

"They say the folks east of here aren't doing so well with their silkworms. There won't be any reason for the price of leaves to go much higher."

Old Tong Bao recognized the speaker as Sixth Treasure, and he relaxed still further.

The girl and A Duo were standing beside a large basket, stripping leaves. In the dim starlight, they worked quite close to each other,

「地頭上還有十擔葉，夠一天。」

阿四回答，他委實是支撐不住了，他的一雙眼皮像有幾百斤重，只想合下來。老通寶卻不耐煩了，怒聲喝道：

「說什麼夢話！剛吃了兩天老蠶呢。明天不算，還得吃三天，還要三十擔葉，三十擔！」

這時外邊稻場上忽然人聲喧鬧，阿多押了新發來的五擔葉來了。於是老通寶和阿四的談話打斷，都出去「捋葉」。四大娘也慌忙從蠶房裏鑽出來。隔溪陸家養的蠶不多，那大姑娘六寶抽得出工夫，也來幫忙了。那時星光滿天，微微有點風，村前村後都斷斷續續傳來了吆喝和歡笑，中間有一個粗暴的聲音嚷道：

「葉行情飛漲了！今天下午鎮上開到四洋一擔！」

老通寶偏偏聽得了，心裏急得什麼似的。四塊錢一擔，三十擔可要一百二十塊呢，他哪來這許多錢！但是想到繭子總可以採五百多斤，就算五十塊錢一百斤，也有這麼二百五，他又心裏一寬。那邊「捋葉」的人堆裏忽然又有一個小小的聲音說：

「聽說東路不大好，看來葉價錢漲不到多少的！」

老通寶認得這聲音是陸家的六寶。這使他心裏又一寬。

那六寶是和阿多同站在一個筐子邊「捋葉」。在半明半暗的星光下，她和阿多靠得很近。忽然她覺得在那「槓條」的隱蔽下，有一隻

partly hidden by the pile of mulberry branches before them. Suddenly, Sixth Treasure felt someone pinch her thigh. She knew well enough who it was, and she suppressed a giggle. But when, a moment later, a hand brushed against her breasts, she jumped; a little shriek escaped her.

"Aiya!"

"What's wrong?" demanded A Si's wife, working on the other side of the basket.

Sixth Treasure's face flamed scarlet. She shot a glance at A Duo, then quickly lowered her head and resumed stripping leaves. "Nothing," she replied. "I think a caterpillar bit me!"

A Duo bit his lips to keep from laughing aloud. He had been half starved the past two weeks and had slept little. But in spite of having lost a lot of weight, he was in high spirits. While he never suffered from any of Old Tong Bao's gloom, neither did he believe that one good crop, whether of silkworms or of rice, would enable them to wipe off their debt and own their own land again. He knew they would never "get out from under" merely by relying on hard work, even if they broke their backs trying. Nevertheless, he worked with a will. He enjoyed work, just as he enjoyed fooling around with Sixth Treasure.

The next morning, Old Tong Bao went into town to borrow money for more leaves. Before leaving home, he had talked the matter over with daughter-in-law. They had decided to mortgage their grove of mulberries that produced fifteen loads of leaves a year as security for the loan. The grove was the last piece of property the family owned.

By the time the old man ordered another thirty loads, and the first ten were delivered, the sturdy "little darlings" had gone hungry for half an hour. Putting forth their pointed little mouths, they swayed from side to side, searching for food. Daughter-in-law's heart had ached

手在她大腿上擰了一把。好像知道是誰擰的，她忍住了不笑，也不聲張。驀地那手又在她胸前摸了一把，六寶直跳起來，出驚地喊了一聲：

「噯喲！」

「什麼事？」

同在那筐子邊捋葉的四大娘問了，抬起頭來。六寶覺得自己臉上熱烘烘了，她偷偷地瞪了阿多一眼，就趕快低下頭，很快地捋葉，一面回答：

「沒有什麼。想來是毛毛蟲刺了我一下。」

阿多咬住了嘴唇暗笑。雖然在這半個月來也是半飽而且少睡，也瘦了許多了，他的精神可還是很飽滿。老通寶那種憂愁，他是永遠沒有的。他永不相信靠一次蠶花好或是田裏熟，他們就可以還清了債再有自己的田；他知道單靠勤儉工作，即使做到背脊骨折斷也是不能翻身的。但是他仍舊很高興地工作着，他覺得這也是一種快活，正像和六寶調情一樣。

第二天早上，老通寶就到鎮裏去想法借錢來買葉。臨走前，他和四大娘商量好，決定把他家那塊出產十五擔葉的桑地去抵押。這是他家最後的產業。

葉又買來了三十擔。第一批的十擔發來時，那些壯健的「寶寶」已經餓了半點鐘了。「寶寶」們尖出了小嘴巴，向左向右亂晃，四大

to see them. When the leaves were finally spread in the trays, the silk-worm shed at once resounded with a sibilant crunching, so noisy it drowned out conversation. In a very short while, the trays were again empty of leaves. Another thick layer was piled on. Just keeping the silkworms supplied with leaves, Old Tong Bao and his family were so busy they could barely catch their breath. But this was the final crisis. In two more days the "little darlings" would spin their cocoons. People were putting every bit of their remaining strength into this last desperate struggle.

Though he had gone without sleep for three whole days, A Duo didn't appear particularly tired. He agreed to watch the shed alone that night until dawn to permit the others to get some rest. There was a bright moon and the weather was a trifle cold. A Duo crouched beside a small fire he had built in the shed. At about eleven, he gave the silkworms their second feeding, then returned to squat by the fire. He could hear the loud rustle of the "little darlings" crunching through the leaves. His eyes closed. Suddenly, he heard the door squeak, and his eyelids flew open. He peered into the darkness for a moment, then shut his eyes again. His ears were still hissing with the rustle of the leaves. The next thing he knew, his head had struck against his knees. Waking with a start, he heard the door screen bang and thought he saw a moving shadow. A Duo leaped up and rushed outside. In the moonlight, he saw somcone crossing the threshing ground towards the stream. He caught up in a flash, seized and flung the intruder to the ground. A Duo was sure he had nabbed a thief.

"A Duo, kill me if you want to, but don't give me away!"

The voice made A Duo's hair stand on end. He could see in the moonlight that queer flat white face and those round little piggy eyes fixed upon him. But of menace, the piggy eyes had none. A Duo snorted.

娘看得心酸。葉鋪了上去，立刻蠶房裏充滿着薩薩薩的響聲，人們說話也不大聽得清。不多一會兒，那些「團扁」裏立刻又全見白了，於是又鋪上厚厚的一層葉。人們單是「上葉」也就忙得透不過氣來。但這是最後五分鐘了。再得兩天，「寶寶」可以上山。人們把剩餘的精力榨出來拚死命幹。

阿多雖然接連三日三夜沒有睡，卻還不見怎麼倦。那一夜，就由他一個人在「蠶房」裏守那上半夜，好讓老通寶以及阿四夫婦都去歇一歇。那是個好月夜，稍稍有點冷。蠶房裏燃了一個小小的火。阿多守到二更過，上了第二次的葉，就蹲在那個「火」旁邊聽那些「寶寶」薩薩薩地吃葉。漸漸兒他的眼皮合上了。恍惚聽得有門響，阿多的眼皮一跳，睜開眼來看了看，就又合上了。他耳朵裏還聽得薩薩薩的聲音和屑索屑索的怪聲。猛然一個跟蹌，他的頭在自己膝頭上磕了一下，他驚醒過來，恰就聽得蠶房的蘆帘拍又一聲響，似乎還看見有人影一閃。阿多立刻跳起來，到外面一看，門是開着，月光下稻場上有一個人正走向溪邊去。阿多飛也似跳出去，還沒看清那人是誰，已經把那人抓過來摔在地下。他斷定了這是一個賊。

「多多頭！打死我也不怨你，只求你不要說出來！」

是荷花的聲音，阿多聽真了時不禁渾身的汗毛都豎了起來。月光下他又看見那扁得作怪的白臉兒上一對細圓的眼睛定定地看住了他。可是恐怖的意思那眼睛裏也沒有。阿多哼了一聲，就問道：

"What were you after?"

"A few of your family's little darlings'!"

"What did you do with them?"

"Threw them in the stream!"

A Duo's face darkened. He knew that in this way she was trying to put a curse on the lot. "You're pure poison! We never did anything to hurt you."

"Never did anything? Oh yes, you did! Yes, you did! Our silkworm eggs didn't hatch well, but we didn't harm anybody. You were all so smart! You shunned me like a leper. No matter how far away I was, if you saw me, you turned your heads. You acted as if I wasn't even human!"

She got to her feet, the agonized expression on her face terrible to see. A Duo stared at her. "I'm not going to beat you," he said finally. "Go on your way!"

Without giving her another glance, he trotted back to the shed. He was wide awake now. Lotus had only taken a handful and the remaining "little darlings" were all in good condition. It didn't occur to him either to hate or pity Lotus, but the last thing she had said remained in his mind. It seemed to him there was something eternally wrong in the scheme of human relations; but he couldn't put his finger on what it was excatly, nor did he know why it should be. In a little while, he forgot about this too. The lusty silkworms were eating and eating, yet, as if by some magic, never full!

Nothing more happened that night. Just before the sky began to brighten in the east, Old Tong Bao and his daughter-in-law came to relieve A Duo. They took the trays of "little darlings" and looked at them in the light. The silkworms were turning a whiter colour, their

「你偷什麼？」

「我偷你們的寶寶！」

「放到哪裏去了？」

「我扔到溪裏去了！」

阿多現在也變了臉色。他這才知道這女人的惡意是要沖克他家的「寶寶」。

「你真心毒呀！我們家和你們可沒有冤仇！」

「沒有麼？有的，有的！我家自管蠶花不好，可並沒害了誰，你們都是好的！你們怎麼把我當作白老虎，遠遠地望見我就別轉了臉？你們不把我當人看待！」

那婦人說着就爬了起來，臉上的神氣比什麼都可怕。阿多瞅着那婦人好半晌，這才說道：

「我不打你，走你的罷！」

阿多頭也不回的跑回家去，仍在「蠶房」裏守着。他完全沒有睡意了。他看那些「寶寶」，都是好好的。他並沒想到荷花可恨或可憐，然而他不能忘記荷花那一番話；他覺到人和人中間有什麼地方是永遠弄不對的，可是他不能夠明白想出來是什麼地方，或是為什麼。再過一會兒，他就什麼都忘記了。「寶寶」是強健的，像有魔法似的吃了又吃，永遠不會飽！

以後直到東方快打白了時，沒有發生事故。老通寶和四大娘來替換阿多了，他們拿那些漸漸身體發白而變短了的「寶寶」在亮處照

bodies gradually becoming shorter and thicker. They were delighted with the excellent way the silkworms were developing.

But when, at sunrise, A Si's wife went to draw water at the stream, she met Sixth Treasure. The girl's expression was serious.

"I saw that slut leaving your place shortly before midnight," she whispered. "A Duo was right behind her. They stood here and talked for a long time! Your family ought to look after things better than that!"

The colour drained from the face of A Si's wife. Without a word, she carried her water bucket back to the house. First she told her husband about it, then she told Old Tong Bao. It was a fine state of affairs when a baggage like that could sneak into people's silkworm sheds! Old Tong Bao stamped with rage. He immediately summoned A Duo. But the boy denied the whole story; he said Sixth Treasure was dreaming. The old man then went to question Sixth Treasure. She insisted she had seen everything with her own eyes. The old man didn't know what to believe. He returned home and looked at the "little darlings." They were as sturdy as ever, not a sickly one in the lot.

But the joy that old Tong Bao and his family had been feeling was dampened. They knew Sixth Treasure's words couldn't be entirely without foundation. Their only hope was that A Duo and that hussy had played their little games on the porch rather than in the shed!

Old Tong Bao recalled gloomily that the garlic had only put forth three or four shoots. He thought the future looked dark. Hadn't there been times before when the silkworms ate great quantities of leaves and seemed to be growing well, yet dried up and died just when they were ready to spin their cocoons? Yes, often! But Old Tong Bao didn't dare let himself think of such a possibility. To entertain a thought like that, even in the most secret recesses of the mind, would only be inviting bad luck!

着，看是「有沒有通」。他們的心被快活脹大了。但是太陽出山時四大娘到溪邊汲水，卻看見六寶滿臉嚴重地跑過來悄悄地問道：

「昨夜二更過，三更不到，我遠遠地看見那騷貨從你們家跑出來，阿多跟在後面，他們站在這裏說了半天話呢！四阿嫂！你們怎麼不管事呀？」

四大娘的臉色立刻變了，一句話也沒說，提了水桶就回家去，先對丈夫說了，再對老通寶說。這東西竟偷進人家「蠶房」來了，那還了得！老通寶氣得直跺腳，馬上叫了阿多來查問。但是阿多不承認，說六寶是做夢見鬼。老通寶又去找六寶詢問。六寶是一口咬定了看見的。老通寶沒有主意，回家去看那「寶寶」，仍然是很健康，瞧不出一些敗相來。

但是老通寶他們滿心的歡喜卻被這件事打消了。他們相信六寶的話不會毫無根據。他們唯一的希望是那騷貨或者只在廊簷口和阿多鬼混了一陣。

「可是那大蒜頭上的苗卻當真只有三四莖呀！」

老通寶自心裏這麼想，覺得前途只是陰暗。可不是，吃了許多葉去，一直落來都很好，然而上了山卻乾殭了的事，也是常有的。不過老通寶無論如何不敢想到這上頭去；他以為即使是肚子裏想，也是不吉利。

IV

The "little darlings" began spinning their cocoons, but Old Tong Bao's family was still in a sweat. Both their money and their energy were completely spent. They still had nothing to show for it; there was no guarantee of their earning any return. Nevertheless, they continued working at top speed. Beneath the racks on which the cocoons were being spun fires had to be kept going to supply warmth. Old Tong Bao and A Si, his elder son, their backs bent, slowly squatted first on this side then on that. Hearing the small rustlings of the spinning silkworms, they wanted to smile, and if the sounds stopped for a moment their hearts stopped too. Yet, worried as they were, they didn't dare to disturb the silkworms by looking inside. When the silkworms squirted fluid in their faces as they peered up from beneath the racks, they were happy in spite of the momentary discomfort. The bigger the shower, the better they liked it.

A Duo had already peeked several times. Little Bao had caught him at it and demanded to know what was going on. A Duo made an ugly face at the child, but did not reply.

After three days of "spinning," the fires were extinguished. A Si's wife could restrain herself no longer. She stole a look, her heart beating fast. Inside, all was white as snow. The brush that had been put in for the silkworms to spin on was completely covered over with cocoons. A Si's wife had never seen so successuful a "flowering" !

The whole family was wreathed in smiles. They were on solid ground at last! The "little darlings" had proved they had a conscience; they hadn't consumed those mulberry leaves, at four dollars a load, in

四

「寶寶」都上山了，老通寶他們還是捏着一把汗。他們錢都花光了，精力也絞盡了，可是有沒有報酬呢，到此時還沒有把握。雖則如此，他們還是硬着頭皮去幹。「山棚」下爇了火，老通寶和阿四他們傴着腰慢慢地從這邊蹲到那邊，又從那邊蹲到這邊。他們聽得山棚上有些屑屑索索的細聲音，他們就忍不住想笑，過一會兒又不聽得了，他們的心就重甸甸地往下沉了。這樣地，心是焦灼着，卻不敢向山棚上望。偶或他們仰着的臉上淋到了一滴蠶尿了，雖然覺得有點難過，他們心裏卻快活；他們巴不得多淋一些。

阿多早已偷偷地挑開「山棚」外圍着的蘆帘望過幾次了。小小寶看見，就扭住了阿多，問「寶寶」有沒有做繭子。阿多伸出舌頭做一個鬼臉，不回答。

「上山」後三天，息火了。四大娘再也忍不住，也偷偷地挑開蘆帘角看了一眼，她的心立刻卜卜地跳了。那是一片雪白，幾乎連「綴頭」都瞧不見；那是四大娘有生以來從沒有見過的「好蠶花」呀！老通寶全家立刻充滿了歡笑。現在他們一顆心定下來了！「寶寶」們有良

vain. The family could reap its reward for a month of hunger and sleepless nights. The Old Lord of the Sky had eyes!

Throughout the village, there were many similar scenes of rejoicing. The Silkworm Goddess had been beneficent to the tiny village this year. Most of the two dozen families garnered good crops of cocoons from their silkworms. The harvest of Old Tong Bao's family was well above average.

Again women and children crowded the threshing ground and the banks of the little stream. All were much thinner than the previous month, with eyes sunk in their sockets, throats rasping and hoarse. But everyone was excited, happy. As they chattered about the struggle of the past month, visions of piles of bright silver dollars shimmered before their eyes. Cheerful thoughts filled their minds — they would get their summer clothes out of the pawnshop; at Dragon-Boat Festival perhaps they could eat a fat golden fish....

They talked, too, of the farce enacted by Lotus and A Duo a few nights before. Sixth Treasure announced to everyone she met, "That Lotus has no shame at all. She delivered herself right to his door!" Men who heard her laughed coarsely. Women muttered a prayer and called Lotus bad names. They said Old Tong Bao's family could consider itself lucky that a curse hadn't fallen on them. The gods were merciful!

Family after family was able to report a good harvest of cocoons. People visited one another to view the shining white gossamer. The father of Old Tong Bao's daughter-in-law came from town with his little son. They brought gifts of sweets and fruits and a salted fish. Little Bao was happy as a puppy frolicking in the snow.

The elderly visitor sat with Old Tong Bao beneath a willow beside the stream. He had the reputation in town of a "man who knew how to enjoy life." From hours of listening to the professional story-tellers

心，四洋一擔的葉不是白吃的；他們全家一個月的忍餓失眠總算不冤枉，天老爺有眼睛！

同樣的歡笑聲在村裏到處都起來了。今年蠶花娘娘保祐這小小的村子。二三十人家都可以採到七八分，老通寶家更是比眾不同，估量來總可以採一個十二三分。

小溪邊和稻場上現在又充滿了女人和孩子們。這些人都比一個月前瘦了許多，眼眶陷進了，嗓子也發沙，然而都很快活興奮。她們嘈嘈地談論那一個月內的「奮鬥」時，她們的眼前便時時現出一堆堆雪白的洋錢，她們那快樂的心裏便時時閃過了這樣的盤算：夾衣和夏衣都在當鋪裏，這可先得贖出來；過端陽節也許可以吃一條黃魚。

那晚上荷花和阿多的把戲也是她們談話的資料。六寶見了人就宣傳荷花的「不要臉，送上門去！」男人們聽了就粗暴地笑着，女人們唸一聲佛，罵一句，又說老通寶家總算幸氣，沒有犯克，那是菩薩保祐，祖宗有靈！

接着是家家都「浪山頭」了，各家的至親好友都來「望山頭」。老通寶的親家張財發帶了小兒子阿九特地從鎮上來到村裏。他們帶來的禮物，是軟糕、線粉、梅子、枇杷，也有鹹魚。小小寶快活得好像雪天的小狗。

「通寶，你是賣繭子呢，還是自家做絲？」

張老頭子拉老通寶到小溪邊一棵楊柳樹下坐了，這麼悄悄地問。這張老頭子張財發是出名「會尋快活」的人，他從鎮上城隍廟前露天的「說書場」聽來了一肚子的疙瘩東西；尤其爛熟的，是「十八路

in front of the temple, he had learned by heart many of the classic tales of ancient times. He was a great one for idle chatter, and often would say anything that came into his head. Old Tong Bao therefore didn't take him very seriously when he leaned close and queried softly:

"Are you selling your cocoons, or will you spin the silk yourself at home?"

"Selling them, of course," Old Tong Bao replied casually.

The elderly visitor slapped his thigh and sighed, then rose abruptly and pointed at the silk filature rearing up behind the row of mulberries, now quite bald of leaves.

"Tong Bao," he said, "the cocoons are being gathered, but the doors of the silk filatures are shut as tight as ever! They're not buying this year! Ah, all the world is in turmoil! The silk houses are not going to open, I tell you!"

Old Tong Bao couldn't help smiling. He wouldn't believe it. How could he possibly believe it? There were dozens of silk filatures in this part of the country. Surely they couldn't all shut down? What's more, he had heard that they had made a deal with the Japanese; the Chinese soliders who had been billeted in the silk houses had long since departed.

Changing the subject, the visitor related the latest town gossip, salting it freely with classical aphorisms and quotations from the ancient stories. Finally he got around to the thirty silver dollars borrowed through him as middleman. He said his boss was anxious to be repaid.

Old Tong Bao became uneasy after all. When his visitor had departed, he hurried from the village down the highway to look at the two nearest silk filatures. Their doors were indeed shut; not a soul was in sight. Business was in full swing this time last year, with whole rows of dark gleaming scales in operation.

反王，七十二處煙塵」，程咬金賣柴扒，販私鹽出身，瓦崗寨做反王的《隋唐演義》。他向來說話「沒正經」，老通寶是知道的；所以現在聽得問是賣繭子或者自家做絲，老通寶並沒把這話看重，只隨口回答道：

「自然賣繭子。」

張老頭子卻拍着大腿嘆一口氣。忽然他站了起來，用手指着村外那一片禿頭桑林後面聳露出來的繭廠的風火牆說道：

「通寶！繭子是採了，那些繭廠的大門還關得緊洞洞呢！今年繭廠不開秤！——十八路反王早已下凡，李世民還沒出世；世界不太平！今年繭廠關門，不做生意！」

老通寶忍不住笑了，他不肯相信。他怎麼能夠相信呢？難道那「五步一崗」似的比露天毛坑還要多的繭廠會一齊都關了門不做生意？況且聽說和東洋人也已「講攏」，不打仗了，繭廠裏駐的兵早已開走。

張老頭子也換了話，東拉西扯講鎮裏的「新聞」，夾着許多「說書場」上聽來的什麼秦叔寶，程咬金。最後，他代他的東家催那三十塊錢的債，為的他是「中人」。

然而老通寶到底有點不放心。他趕快跑出村去，看看「塘路」上最近的兩個繭廠，果然大門緊閉，不見半個人；照往年說，此時應該早已擺開了櫃台，掛起了一排烏亮亮的大秤。

He felt a little panicky as he returned home. But when he saw those snowy cocoons, thick and hard, pleasure made him smile. What beauties! No one wants them? — Impossible. He still had to hurry and finish gathering the cocoons; he hadn't thanked the gods properly yet. Gradually, he forgot about the silk houses.

But in the village, the atmosphere was changing day by day. People who had just begun to laugh were now all frowns. News was reaching them from town that none of the neighbouring silk filatures was opening its doors. It was the same with the houses along the highway. Last year at this time buyers of cocoons were streaming in and out of the village. This year there wasn't a sign of even half a one. In their place came dunning creditors and government tax collectors who promptly froze up if you asked them to take cocoons in payment.

Swearing, curses, disappointed sighs! With such a fine crop of cocoons the villagers had never dreamed that their lot would be even worse than usual! It was as if hailstones dropped out of a clear sky. People like Old Tong Bao, whose crop was especially good, took it hardest of all.

"What is the world coming to!" He beat his breast and stamped his feet in helpless frustration.

But the villagers had to think of something. The cocoons would spoil if kept too long. They either had to sell them or remove the silk themselves. Several families had already brought out and repaired silk reels they hadn't used for years. They would first remove the silk from the cocoons and then see about the next step. Old Tong Bao wanted to do the same.

"We won't sell our cocoons; we'll spin the silk ourselves!" said the old man. "Nobody ever heard of selling cocoons until the foreign devils' companies started the thing!"

老通寶心裏也着慌了，但是回家去看見了那些雪白發光很厚實硬鼓鼓的繭子，他又忍不住嘻開了嘴。上好的繭子！會沒有人要，他不相信。並且他還要忙着採繭，還要謝「蠶花利市」，他漸漸不把繭廠的事放在心上了。

可是村裏的空氣一天一天不同了。才得笑了幾聲的人們現在又都是滿臉的愁雲。各處繭廠都沒開門的消息陸續從鎮上傳來，從「塘路」上傳來。往年這時候，「收繭人」像走馬燈似的在村裏巡迴，今年沒見半個「收繭人」，卻換替着來了債主和催糧的差役。請債主們就收了繭子罷，債主們板起面孔不理。

全村子都是嚷罵，詛咒，和失望的嘆息！人們做夢也不會想到今年「蠶花」好了，他們的日子卻比往年更加困難。這在他們是一個青天的霹靂！並且愈是像老通寶他們家似的，蠶愈養得多，愈好，就愈加困難，——「真正世界變了！」老通寶捶胸跺腳地沒有辦法。然而繭子是不能擱久了的，總得趕快想法：不是賣出去，就是自家做絲。村裏有幾家已經把多年不用的絲車拿出來修理，打算自家把繭做成了絲再說。六寶家也打算這麼辦。老通寶便也和兒子媳婦商量道：

「不賣繭子了，自家做絲！什麼賣繭子，本來是洋鬼子行出來的！」

A Si's wife was the first to object. "We've got over five hundred catties of cocoons here," she retorted. "Where are you going to get enough reels?"

She was right. Five hundred catties was no small amount. They'd never get finished spinning the silk themselves. Hire outside help? That meant spending money. A Si agreed with his wife. A Duo blamed his father for planning incorrectly.

"If you listened to me, we'd have raised only one tray of foreign breed and no locals. Then the fifteen loads of leaves from our own mulberry trees would have been enough, and we wouldn't have had to borrow!"

Old Tong Bao was so angry he couldn't speak.

At last a ray of hope appeared. Huang the Priest had heard somewhere that a silk house below the city of Wuxi was doing business as usual. Actually an ordinary peasant, Huang was nicknamed "The Priest" because of the learned airs he affected and his interests in Taoist "magic." Old Tong Bao always got along with him fine. After learning the details from him, Old Tong Bao conferred with his elder son A Si about going to Wuxi.

"It's about 270 *li* by water, six days for the round trip," ranted the old man. "Son of a bitch! It's a goddam expedition! But what else can we do? We can't eat the cocoons, and our creditors are pressing hard!"

A Si agreed. They borrowed a small boat and bought a few yards of matting to cover the cargo. It was decided that A Duo should go along. Taking advantage of the good weather, the cocoon selling "expeditionary force" set out.

Five days later, the men returned — but not with an empty hold. They still had one basket of cocoons. The silk filature, which they

「我們有四百多斤繭子呢，你打算擺幾部絲車呀！」

四大娘首先反對了。她這話是不錯的。五百斤的繭子可不算少，自家做絲萬萬幹不了。請幫手麼？那又得花錢。阿四是和他老婆一條心。阿多抱怨老頭子打錯了主意，他說：

「早依了我的話，扣住自己的十五擔葉，只看一張洋種，多麼好！」

老通寶氣得說不出話來。

終於一線希望忽又來了。同村的黃道士不知從哪裏得的消息，說是無錫腳下的繭廠還是照常收繭。黃道士也是一樣的種田人，並非吃十方的「道士」，向來和老通寶最說得來。於是老通寶去找那黃道士詳細問過了以後，便又和兒子阿四商量把繭子弄到無錫腳下去賣。老通寶虎起了臉，像吵架似的嚷道：

「水路去有三十多九呢！來回得六天！他媽的！簡直是充軍！可是你有別的辦法麼？繭子當不得飯吃，蠶前的債又逼緊來！」

阿四也同意了。他們去借了一條赤膊船，買了幾張蘆席，趁那幾天正是好晴，又帶了阿多。他們這賣繭子的「遠征軍」就此出發。

五天以後，他們果然回來了；但不是空船，船裏還有一筐繭子

reached after a 270-*li* journey by water, offered extremely harsh terms — Only thirty-five dollars a load for foreign breed, twenty for local; thin cocoons not wanted at any price. Although their cocoons were all first class, the people at the silk house picked and chose, leaving them one basket of rejects. Old Tong Bao and his sons received a hundred and ten dollars for the sale, ten of which had to be spent as travel expenses. The hundred dollars remaining was not even enough to pay back what they had borrowed for that last thirty loads of mulberry leaves! On the return trip, Old Tong Bao became ill with rage. His sons carried him into the house.

A Si's wife had no choice but to take the ninety odd catties they had brought back and reel the silk from the cocoons herself. She borrowed a few reels from Sixth Treasure's family and worked for six days. All their rice was gone now. A Si took the silk into town, but no one would buy it. Even the pawnshop didn't want it. Only after much pleading was he able to persuade the pawnbroker to take it in exchange for a load of rice they had pawned before Clear and Bright.

That's the way it happened. Because they raised a crop of spring silkworms, the people in Old Tong Bao's village got deeper into debt. Old Tong Bao's family raised five trays and gathered a splendid harvest of cocoons. Yet they ended up owing another thirty silver dollars and losing their mortgaged mulberry trees — to say nothing of suffering a month of hunger and sleepless nights in vain!

November 1, 1932

沒有賣出。原來那三十多九水路遠的繭廠挑剔得非常苛刻：洋種繭一擔只值三十五元，土種繭一擔二十元，薄繭不要。老通寶他們的繭子雖然是上好的貨色，卻也被繭廠裏挑剩了那麼一筐，不肯收買。老通寶他們實賣得一百十一塊錢，除去路上盤川，就剩了整整的一百元，不夠償還買青葉所借的債！老通寶路上氣得生病了，兩個兒子扶他到家。

打回來的八九十斤繭子，四大娘只好自家做絲了。她到六寶家借了絲車，又忙了五六天。家裏米又吃完了。叫阿四拿那絲上鎮裏去賣，沒有人要；上當鋪當鋪也不收。説了多少好話，總算把清明前當在那裏的一石米換了出來。

就是這麼着，因為春蠶熟，老通寶一村的人都增加了債！老通寶家為的養了五張布子的蠶，又採了十多分的好繭子，就此白賠上十五擔葉的桑地和三十塊錢的債！一個月光景的忍餓熬夜還都不算！

1932年11月1日